JENNY VILLIERS

BY J. B. PRIESTLEY

FICTION

BRIGHT DAY

THREE MEN IN NEW SUITS

DAYLIGHT ON SATURDAY

BLACK-OUT IN GRETLEY

LET THE PEOPLE SING

THE DOOMSDAY MEN

THEY WALK IN THE CITY

FARAWAY

ANGEL PAVEMENT

THE GOOD COMPANIONS

WONDER HERO

BENIGHTED

ADAM IN MOONSHINE

JENNY VILLIERS

PLAYS

THREE COMEDIES
Goodnight Children
How Are They at Home
The Golden Fleece

THREE PLAYS
Music at Night
The Long Valley
They Came to a City

JOHNSON OVER JORDAN

I HAVE BEEN HERE BEFORE

TIME AND THE CONWAYS

WHEN WE ARE MARRIED

BEES ON THE BOAT DECK

DUET IN FLOODLIGHT

CORNELIUS

EDEN END

DANGEROUS CORNER

LABURNUM GROVE

THE ROUNDABOUT

AN INSPECTOR CALLS

MISCELLANEOUS

POSTSCRIPTS

RAIN UPON GODSHILL

MIDNIGHT ON THE DESERT

ENGLISH JOURNEY

FOUR-IN-HAND

I FOR ONE

TALKING: AN ESSAY

OPEN HOUSE

APES AND ANGELS

SELF-SELECTED ESSAYS

THE BALCONINNY

THE ENGLISH COMIC CHARACTER

MEREDITH (E.M.L.)

PEACOCK (E.M.L.)

THE ENGLISH NOVEL

HUMOUR (E. HERITAGE SERIES)

BRIEF DIVERSIONS

JENNY VILLIERS

A Story of the Theatre

BY

J. B. PRIESTLEY

WILLIAM HEINEMANN LTD
LONDON :: TORONTO

DRAWINGS BY MISS M. ELAINE HANCOCK

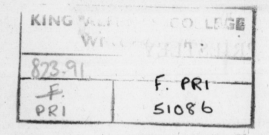

FIRST PUBLISHED 1947
—
PRINTED IN GREAT BRITAIN AT THE WINDMILL PRESS
KINGSWOOD, SURREY

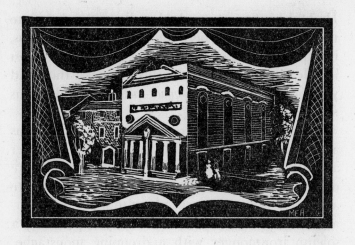

I

THERE are two ways into the famous Green Room of the Theatre Royal, Barton Spa. Coming from the front of the house, you go behind the dress circle and then along a corridor, past the manager's office. From backstage you climb a dark flight of stairs just beyond the two star dressing-rooms. Martin Cheveril, having entered the theatre by the stage door, was now at the top of this dark flight of stairs, and although the door into the Green Room was closed, he could hear the idiotic *quack-quack-quack* of the cocktail party in there.

I

He had his fingers on the handle of the door into the Green Room, where the party was in progress, but instead of opening the door he leaned against it. He felt worse now, deathly weary, a thousand years old. *Quack-quack-quack-quack.* God help us all!

Then they stopped quacking, just as he was about to force himself to turn that handle. After all, although he had his excuse ready, it was more or less his party. There was now some polite applause. Somebody was about to make a speech, and ten to one it would be the Mayor, probably a solemn ironmonger with a drooping moustache. Yes, this was the Mayor, and, like so many municipal orators, he insisted upon giving every word the same weight and value.

"On behalf of the Borough Council of Barton Spa," Cheveril could hear him declaring, "I 'ave very great pleasure in welcoming to our ancient borough—the very talented actors an' actresses who 'ave come with Mr. Cheveril from London—to give us 'ere in Barton Spa—the first performance of 'is new play—*The*—er *The Glass Door.*" And the Mayor sounded rather surprised when he finally pronounced the title. Glum in his dusk behind the door, and feeling like a ghost, Cheveril told the Mayor, in the huge pause that followed, that His Worship would be more

2

surprised still before Cheveril and his Glass Door
had done with him.

"We are looking forward—very much—to seeing
this piece before London sees it," the Mayor
continued, playing each word like an ace of
trumps. "And I'm sure Mr. Cheveril and 'is
company will find 'ere as good an audience as they
can 'ope to find anywhere—very keen an' always
ready for a good laugh."

And I'll bet they are, Cheveril told himself,
while the party broke in with a few good laughs of
its own and some scattered applause. No doubt
all ready to giggle their heads off. But wait until
he had finished with them.

"Now we people in Barton Spa," the Mayor
intoned, clearly about to strike a richer seam, "are
very proud of this old Theatre Royal of ours—
which dates back nearly two 'undred years—and
'as been associated with some of the greatest
actors an' actresses of its time. We've spent a good
deal of time an' trouble—yes, *and* money—keepin'
this famous old theatre—including the old Green
Room 'ere—in good shape—keeping everything
we could keep—to remind us that this is one of the
oldest theatres in the country. A lot of people
think it's the best outside London. We *know* it is."

Some laughter and more applause here. Fair
enough too, Cheveril thought; for this was a fine

3

old theatre, one of the best of its kind, and the Green Room itself was unique, deserving more than the casual reference that the Mayor gave it. An enchanting old room, once you had emptied the idiotic cocktail party out of it.

"Well," said the Mayor, "I 'ope you ladies an' gentleman who 'ave come to entertain us will accept our best wishes for the show—an' that you'll 'ave a very enjoyable stay—so you'll want to come again." More applause. Evidently this was all the Mayor had to say. And if Cheveril was going in to reply, this was the moment. But he remained where he was.

"Ladies and gentlemen——" and this sounded like the little manager, Otley—"as Mr. Cheveril has been delayed, I'm going to ask Miss Pauline Fraser, leading lady of *The Glass Door* Company, to reply on his behalf."

Well, Pauline would do it very nicely, in her best *Thank-you-dear-audience* voice, with a demure mouth but with a roguish sparkling look, all glossy well-tailored charm. Yes, here it came, and sounding as false as hell in this dusk behind the door.

" . . . Must apologise for the absence of Mr. Cheveril . . . know how sorry he'll be that he's missed this lovely party. . . . All of us in the Company *do* appreciate the privilege of playing in this beautiful old theatre of yours . . ." Some

4

applause here, neat and professional applause, from the rest of the company. Pauline went on: "We've all heard and read about the famous old Theatre Royal of Barton Spa—and of this old Green Room you've kept so wonderfully. It has a lovely atmosphere, even if at times it *is* a bit ghostly."

A few laughs for this, of course, but it was true enough, Cheveril reflected. So far he had been too busy with the play to do more than glance round that Green Room, but even so he felt that the place had an atmosphere. And to-night he might have time to discover how rich and deep that atmosphere was, if they would only leave him alone in there for an hour or two. But perhaps he felt it more because he was now in this brown dusk, like that of a thickly-varnished old painting, and half a ghost himself, thinning out, dusk creeping in toward his bones.

"Being here," cried Pauline, with her usual fine diction, "in this old place with a brand-new play, which we'll have to rehearse again to-night—so I hope nobody's had too many cocktails——" all nicely timed for the laugh, which came promptly—— "I say, being here makes me feel all over again what a marvellous thing the Theatre is." She was off now, with strings in unison and woodwind added. "Never as good as it was—always just about to die—but somehow always renewing its enchantment—always finding new life—perhaps just because it's so warm and human, so foolish and yet so glorious—as people themselves are. Yes, just because it's really so close to the heart. That's why we're all so glad and proud to be working for it. And we're so glad and proud to be here. Thank you very much."

This was the moment, while they were clapping. So in he went, clapping like the rest of them, but slower, with irony. The Green Room filled with people was bright and hot, with a thick monkey house atmosphere; and he found himself shrinking, turning cold, very dry and ancient, not really a dramatist of fifty but a Taoist hermit nearly as old as his cave among the remote blue hills. Perhaps nobody would notice him, that thinning out having gone much too far. Plenty of too solid flesh in here, all flavoured with Martinis.

Little Otley, who was in charge, living gloriously, and noticing everything, saw him first. "Mr. Cheveril!" he cried, darting forward, red and ripe.

Pauline, tall and handsome in black, whirled round, and forgot that half Barton Spa was still there. "Martin—you brute!—you were listening." There were some laughs, more clapping, cries of "Speech," and Otley held up a hand.

"Mr. Cheveril," he announced, "has arrived

6

just in time to miss the drinks but not too late to say a few words. Mr. Martin Cheveril."

Fifty or sixty pairs of eyes, some round, some narrowed, but all expectant. Should he give them half a minute of *blah-blah* or tell them what had been passing through his mind, which if they didn't like, then they could lump? He faced them, half embarrassed, half ironical. All right—let them have it, them and their *always ready for a good laugh*. It would require more energy than he had to spare —just standing there, facing their stares, was a terrible effort—but he called up the Old Guard, as he had had to do more than once lately; and then he spoke in an easy but dry tone, clearly the master of the situation.

"I was fortunate enough to overhear Miss Fraser's very charming speech," he told them, after acknowledging the presence of the Mayor and prominent citizenry. "And now I feel it is hardly necessary for me to apologise for not being here earlier. She replied for us all so much better than I could have done." So far, so good; and now to wipe that slightly glazed look off their faces. "But I am not so sure that I agree with what she has said about the Theatre. I'm beginning to have serious doubts whether the Theatre can renew its life and its old enchantments. The play we are opening here, *The Glass Door*, is not only the last

7

play I have written but may well be the last play I shall ever write."

This brought noises, perhaps murmurs of surprise and consternation, and perhaps just noises. Well, it didn't matter tuppence either way. But he had time to notice that Pauline was frowning at him. Poor Pauline!

"And perhaps I had better warn you," he continued, smoother than ever, he hoped, "after this talk of good laughs and warm hearts, that *The Glass Door* is a serious attempt to write about the world as it is and people as they actually are, which means that it may seem to you a grim and rather unpleasant affair, and not what you wanted. If so, please accept my regret in advance." He smiled at them, doing the best he could, though from behind it seemed a tight parchmenty sort of grin. "And I can assure you, Mr. Mayor," he concluded, all rich, warm and false, "that we do appreciate this fine old theatre and the friendly welcome you have offered us. Thank you."

And that, after some rather bewildered applause, broke up the party. The waiters began to clear the tables; the citizens drifted towards one exit and the players towards the other; and Otley introduced Cheveril to the Mayor, who was not moustached Ironmongery but clean-shaven Fancy Goods. Feeling that it was the least he could do, Cheveril

8

accompanied Otley and the Mayor and his body-guard and retinue along the corridor that led to the front of the theatre. This was hard work, and something like penance, for Cheveril felt desperately tired, and was almost aching to sit down. Heaven, he prayed, send me soon a deep chair and no people. Meanwhile from somewhere else there arrived one of those tormentors of the celebrated, a parrot-faced woman who told him that his plays had always been the delight of her life, but who all the time she was talking this fulsome stuff glared at him with suspicious little eyes, like an embittered detective.

"Do you know that woman?" he asked Otley, when they were free at last.

"No, Mr. Cheveril. And I know most people round here."

"I'm not surprised. I've suspected for some time that that kind are not real people at all." He stared mournfully at little Otley. "I think they're demons from hell," he whispered, and then walked slowly back to the Green Room.

9

2

THE waiters and the theatre bar staff had done
a quick neat job. The last remnants of the cocktail
party were now being removed. The Green Room
was almost its sombre but elegant self again.
Three people were standing there, rather close
together; and they were his three leading players:
Pauline Fraser; tall Jimmy Whitefoot, who looked
like a Guards officer and indeed had been one; and
old Alfred Leathers, in his seventies, bulky and
white-haired and wearing the battered, humorous
look shared by retired pugilists and old character

actors. When they saw Cheveril, they contrived at
once, without making any apparent movement, to
be less close together than they had been the
moment before. This told Cheveril that they had
been busy conspiring against him.

Leathers grinned. "How did you leave his
Worship the Mayor?"

"He thinks I'm too modest," Cheveril replied
lightly. "I couldn't persuade him that I meant
what I said about the play."

"Well, I hope you didn't try too hard."

"No," said Cheveril. "I must sit down." And
did, rather heavily. "If you want to start on the
First Act, go ahead. I'll be down later. I have an
appointment with a doctor."

Pauline was alarmed at once. "Martin!"

"No, it's all right. Nothing serious. Same old
thing. Blood pressure down. That's why I
couldn't face that dam' party until the last
minute."

Pauline didn't relax. "Have you seen a doctor
already?"

"Yes. Seemed a sensible sort of chap. He's
looking in with some stuff to keep me going. I'll
be all right." He looked at them with a quizzical
smile. "This could be a deputation."

Leathers was apologetic. "Well, yes, old boy,
you could call it that."

"Go on then." Oh dear! He liked all three of them, and indeed Pauline and dear old Alfred had been his friends for years, but now he wished they were thousands of miles away—on a Pacific island. No, they could stay here, and he would take the Pacific island. He closed his eyes, to enjoy a brief flash of the lagoon; and then opened them wide. "It's the Third Act, isn't it?"

Leathers looked at the other two. "You see, he knew."

"Yes, Martin," said Pauline gravely, "it's the Third Act."

Now it was Jimmy Whitefoot's turn. "We've all been feeling it for several days. But we pretended, even to each other, that it was all right."

"And after the rehearsal this morning, we couldn't keep it up any longer." Pauline gave him a dark but fiery look, and was vehement now. "Martin, we all *hate* that Third Act."

"It's true, old boy," said Leathers sadly.

"Rather late to discover that, isn't it?" Cheveril was dry but not unpleasant. "We open here on Monday."

Pauline swept that away. "Yes, but as it's you— and we've done last-minute changes before— there's still time——" But she hesitated.

"Time to do what?" he asked gently.

"Time to write and rehearse another ending to

your play that isn't so cynical and bitter and—and —*hopeless*. Alfred, Jimmy, you tell him——" And she swung away, clearly upset.

"She's quite right, old boy," said Leathers, with huge solemnity. "In my opinion—and I ought to know after fifty years of it—they'll never take that ending. Too much for 'em altogether, Martin. And if you insist on it, then when we get to town we're in for a flop."

Cheveril took it lightly, feeling too tired to match this giant earnestness. Like all actors off the stage, they over-emphasised their mood, as if they were still playing to an upper circle and gallery. "You may be right, Alfred. But I don't much care. And after all, it'll be a fairly distinguished sort of flop and won't do any of you much harm."

"Just a minute, Martin," said Whitefoot, a nice serious lad. "That's not quite what Pauline and I feel. We feel that even if it does run, it's not going to do people any good. They've had a hard time, and they don't want to be hurt any more—and we feel the same——"

Pauline came charging in. "And what you make your characters say and do isn't *true*. I just don't believe it—and it's all wrong."

"Now wait, Pauline," he said quietly. "You and the others read the play. You and I discussed it."

"Yes, but we didn't realise how absolutely desolating and hopeless that Third Act becomes in production." She was very urgent now. "Of course you knew it. But we didn't. There isn't a glimmer of real understanding left between your people in the end—it's as if each one is mumbling away in a glass case——"

"The play's called *The Glass Door*, you know," he reminded her.

"It might just as well," she cried savagely, "be called *The Glass Coffin*."

The pause that inevitably followed this remark, which a Broadway director would recognise as the pay-off line, was awkward, distinctly awkward. Leathers and Whitefoot exchanged glances. Pauline, not a tearful type, looked as if she might find it easy now to cry; but she made an effort, and said quietly to the two actors: "You'd better go down and start the First Act. Tell Bernard I'll be ready for my entrance."

"All right, my dear," replied Leathers, and marched off with Whitefoot, doing a loud humming that he kept for tricky long exits.

Pauline sat down on a small upright chair not far from the deep armchair that held Cheveril. For several moments she said nothing and did not even look at him. But he looked at her, and thought about her too. How old was she now—

14

forty-five? She didn't look it. Years ago he had
tried to pretend to himself and to her that he was in
love with her, but it hadn't worked: they were
essentially colleagues and friends. Somewhere,
never seen nor mentioned now, there was a
husband; and a boy and a girl still at school and
supported there by Pauline, who also kept her
mother and a vague unsatisfactory sister, always
disappearing into nursing homes. A sound
actress, intelligent and conscientious, perhaps too
intelligent and conscientious, lacking a touch of
strangeness, a hint of unknown dimensions of
being; but well worth the minimum of seventy-five
pounds a week that she demanded. Dark, handsome, capable, and without that bitchy trickiness
which so many actresses are cursed with. He
regarded her with appreciation, with affection too.
But he knew—and disliked himself for it—that the
cold weariness that was lying around his inner self
like an arctic desolation was far beyond her reach,
could not be warmed or illuminated by anything
she said or did, refused to recognise her existence.
So strictly speaking, when she looked at him, as she
did now through a glitter of tears, really he wasn't
there. And what treachery this was to a staunch
colleague, a devoted friend!

"Well, Pauline?"

She was quiet but the emotion was still there,

making her tones uncertain. "It's not only that the
play's going to flop or to hurt people and then
make them harder than ever, but that ending isn't
true. And it isn't really *you*, Martin."

"No, that's where you're wrong. It's me all
right. And I believe it's true." He waited a
moment. "You complain because there's no real
understanding among my characters at the end of
the play. But that's how life is, my dear Pauline. No
real understanding. No genuine communication.
All mumbling and mouthing behind glass doors."

"No," she said, "life's not like that."

He nearly asked her then to look at herself and
him—lovers once, after a fashion—colleagues and
devoted friends for years—and now no understanding, no real communication, a glass wall
between them. But he checked himself, and took
another line. "I don't propose to give our
customers any hotwater bottles and sedatives——"

"I'm not asking you to," she cut in, sharply.

"Let 'em shiver and stay awake—and think for
once, before they start burning and blasting each
other all over again——"

"And they might as well if that's all life is——"

"All right, let 'em." Tempted now, he fell, and
did a bit of showing off. "But this hopeless ending
you hate so much is my parting gift to that cosy,
painted bawdy-house, the Theatre—that nice,

warm, foolish, glorious Theatre you talked about
to the Mayor and Corporation, with its old
enchantment——"

She jumped up, angry. "Stop sneering. That
wasn't a line. I meant it."

"And I mean what *I'm* saying. I'll tell you a
secret, Pauline. In about an hour or so, George
Gavin will be ringing me up from town, and it's
about ten to one he'll offer me joint control of
three of the best theatres in the West End——"

She lit up at once. "Why, that's what you've
always wanted."

"It's what I wanted once. But it comes too late,
like so many things. No proper pattern, no
communication, no real understanding, you see."

"Oh—blow your understandings and patterns!
You're not going to turn down his offer?"

Cheveril grinned. More showing off, of course,
and cheap at that; but he had to enjoy himself
somehow, with that frozen wasteland waiting for
him inside. "That's just what I shall do. With
many thanks. I told you I was through."

She stared at him, horrified, for they had talked
for hours and hours of a chance like this. "Martin,
I don't believe it."

"It's true," he said, this time carefully and
quietly. "I'll go on writing, perhaps a film script
now and then when I need the money, but I shan't

17

go on writing for the Theatre. Not that that matters because I don't think the Theatre, as we know it, will last much longer. The old witchcraft's just about worn out. Oh—I know—I heard you—it's always been just about to die. But don't forget that the most obstinate old invalids do at last turn their faces to the wall. And I believe that's what the Theatre's doing."

"And you don't even *care?*"

"In a way—yes. But not much."

To his surprise, however, she took this quite calmly. She was in fact giving him a long speculative look, with a hint of the clinic about it.

"Just now you don't care about anything very much, do you?" she enquired, out of the clinic.

"No, I don't. I've done most of the things I've wanted to do——"

"No, you haven't. You haven't done the chief thing you ought to have done, the thing you really want to do——"

Cheveril raised his eyebrows. "And what's that?"

"Escaped from your own imprisonment," she told him sharply. "Broken down the glass door you've made for yourself."

"That's what none of us can do." His tone was perhaps a shade too complacent.

"How do *you* know? You don't even know

18

yourself yet." She paused, gave him a dark glance, and then spoke softly. "I know you're not well, Martin—and you're feeling tired and stale—and perhaps I oughtn't to say any more."

"Go on," he said grimly. "I can take it."

"I wonder if you can. You're a tired sick man, Martin."

"Oh—Lord!" He almost shouted in his exasperation. "You'll have me in a bathchair soon. Come on, what is it?"

"The truth about you, Martin—and I've wanted to say this for some time—is that you've been spoilt by success. You've had too much too easily. And because you've nothing—and nobody—to work for, to fight for, to care about, then you're bored and cynical and bitter, and all shut up inside yourself, imagining you know all about life."

He gave this serious consideration, and decided it was quite untrue. Something was wrong, but this was not it. At fifty he was at least fifteen years too old to be accounted for in this fashion. It was clever spoilt young men who were bored and cynical and bitter. He was beyond that nonsense, although he did not blame Pauline for not seeing it. He was immensely and most desolatingly weary, as if most of his energy and all zest for life were drained away somewhere. Probably some gland wasn't functioning properly, a chemical missing. Perhaps

19

the whole engine was running down. But it was no
use going into all that with Pauline, and so he
merely murmured that he knew he'd been lucky
and that it was the millions of poor devils who
hadn't——

"No, it isn't," cried Pauline. "That's just the
point. And that's where you deceive yourself,
Martin. It's nothing to do with other people. It's
you—you. You imagine you've had it all, that
you've nothing to hope for, so everything tastes
stale and sour, and then you invent elaborate
theories to explain it. No communication! Glass
doors!"

"I don't admit that's true," he said mildly. He
knew very well it wasn't. "But suppose it is.
What then? Here I am. How do I change?"

She looked blank, and sounded rather miserable.
"I don't know. It would have to come from deep
down inside. And I don't suppose it ever will,
because now you're all shut off and protected by
your own cleverness and experience." She looked
at him. "Somewhere behind all that cleverness
and experience, and boredom and bitterness,
there's still somebody quite young—and bewildered and disappointed—and lonely—because
he can't talk to anybody, because he's shut up
there alone. I guessed that ten years ago when we
thought we were in love. And I tried to reach

him—to comfort him—and I couldn't—or you wouldn't let me—and so it went all wrong. Oh damn!" The expletive arrived because she did not want to cry but suddenly found herself crying. She turned away, trying to control herself. Cheveril noticed that the back of her neck wobbled rather absurdly, and then thought badly of himself for not feeling more sympathetic. Poor Pauline!

"It's a pretty theory, my dear," he said gently. "But even if it were true, there's obviously nothing to be done about it."

"I know. It's hopeless. It would need a miracle to reach that other Martin Cheveril, shut away there—alone."

"And there aren't any miracles." He waited a moment. "And then you blame me because I end a play with everybody, so to speak, behind glass, making frantic gestures that nobody else understands——"

"No, I don't blame you," she said, out of a vast weariness, as if they had been arguing for years. "And I shan't say anything more to you, Martin. You won't change that hopeless terrible Third Act. You'll leave the Theatre——"

"Which is dying anyhow," he told her.

She turned on him now, with a flash of impatience. "Of course it'll die if people like you leave it." But then she returned to her former tone.

"But I'm thinking about you now—not really writing any more—just passing the time, growing old and hard—and miserable."

The door on the stage side was opened slowly and noisily, and Alfred Leathers looked in. Pauline hastily turned away. "Look, old boy, sorry to butt in," said Leathers, "but we're still getting a nasty little hold-up in that telephone scene in Act One. Bernard has an idea for a cut. Will you come down for a minute and tell us what you think?"

Cheveril said he would, and Leathers vanished. As he passed Pauline, still distressed, Cheveril touched her lightly on the shoulder. "Sorry, Pauline. Take it easy now. They'll be wanting you soon." And he went down to the stage.

3

WHILE Cheveril was down on the stage, first discussing the proposed cut and then watching them run through the new version of the telephone scene two or three times, something happened in the Green Room, and afterwards Pauline told him all about it. She had stayed behind because she had felt she needed a minute or two to herself before facing the rest of the company. She dabbed at her eyes, repaired her make-up, and then, still feeling wobbly, lit a cigarette. This was the first time she had been alone in the Green Room. It was a period room of some charm, fairly large, panelled in dark wood, with many old theatrical portraits on the walls. Two tall glass-fronted cases were filled with costumes, small hand props and odds and ends of historical souvenirs of the theatre. This suggestion of a museum ought to have made the room seem safe and dull enough. But she had not been angling for a laugh when she had said in her speech that it seemed a bit ghostly. It was windowless, shadowy and hidden away, and now that she was alone in it, its atmosphere seemed oppressive, not exactly sinister and menacing, but as if too richly charged with a secret invisible life. After she had lit her cigarette, Pauline tried to concentrate upon Martin Cheveril and to pretend that she was not in the Green Room at all. But it wouldn't have that; and she was about to retreat, quickly too, when there was the sound of voices outside and the door that led to the front of the house was flung open.

A girl darted in, with a harassed Otley, still shouting protests, close behind her. She was an untidy girl wearing a short brown tweed coat and dark green slacks. And Pauline knew at once that she was an actress.

"Oh!" cried the girl, looking round, "he's not here." She was breathless and sounded disappointed.

24

"You see," said Otley, his round red face all
disapproval, "all for nothing. And you ought to be
ashamed of yourself, pushing yourself in like that.
Where would we be if everybody started behaving
like you?"

"I don't know and I don't care," said the girl,
not rude but merely young and desperate. "The
point is, I'm not everybody. I'm an actress—and I
must see Mr. Cheveril."

"Well, you're not going the right way about it,"
Otley told her. Then he turned to Pauline. "I'm
sorry, Miss Fraser. I tried to stop her—but——"

"Oh!" cried the girl, staring with huge round
eyes. She was not a pretty girl, but now Pauline
saw that she had looks of her own, a good stage
face, wide across the cheek-bones, with fine green-
darkish eyes, a perky little nose, and mobile
sensitive lips. "You're Pauline Fraser, aren't you?"

Pauline smiled. "Yes. Who are you?"

"Oh, you've never heard of me. I'm Ann
Seward——"

"Now listen, Miss Seward," Otley began.

But Pauline interrupted him. "No, it's all right,
Mr. Otley. I'm free for a few minutes, and I'll talk
to Miss Seward."

Otley gave it up. "All right, Miss Fraser. I was
only trying to see that Mr. Cheveril wasn't
bothered by anybody."

The girl now gave him an unexpected charming smile. "Of course you were. Sorry—but I just had to come in."

Otley went off grumbling. "I don't know whether you *had* to—but you *are* in——"

Ann Seward turned confidentially to Pauline as soon as Otley had gone. "You see, what happened was this. I'm playing at the Rep. at Wanley, about thirty miles from here, and I heard Mr. Cheveril was trying out his new play here, and I felt I simply *had* to see him. I'm not really like this, though—you know, all pushing and barging in—if I had been, probably I still wouldn't be in weekly Rep."

Pauline smiled at her. "Perhaps not, but still you've plenty of time. You're very young."

This was not Ann's view. "I'm twenty-three," she announced gravely.

"That's not very old."

Ann stared at her with admiration. "I think you're great. When I had a week off, last autumn, I stayed in London and on the Tuesday I went to see you in Martin Cheveril's play, *The Wandering Light.*"

"Good! It was a lovely play."

"Yes. Then I went on Wednesday, and then I went on Thursday. Three times. You were wonderful. But—do you mind if I say this——?"

Pauline was amused. "Probably. But I'll risk it."

The girl was all eagerness, quite unselfconscious now. "Well, at the end of the Second Act, when you get the news that he's back and waiting for you, I think you ought to have dropped everything you were holding—as if it wasn't there any more—and then walked straight out into the garden. Do you mind my saying that?"

"Of course not. As a matter of fact, I wanted to do it like that, only our producer wouldn't let me. Look here—I think you really *are* an actress——"

"Do you?" cried the girl eagerly. "I know I am. Of course it's hopeless in weekly Rep., 'specially in Wanley. I could be a thousand times better if I only had a chance, particularly in a Cheveril play. Please, Miss Fraser, I don't want to be a nuisance—I hated forcing my way in—but I simply had to see him. Where is he?"

"He's down on the stage just now, but he'll be back up here soon. I ought to warn you, though, that he's feeling rather tired and out of sorts and won't want to see anybody——"

"I won't fuss him. I'll just explain quietly who I am and what I've done and ask him to give me a chance."

Pauline nodded. "Well, sit down, and have a cigarette."

"No, thank you. And if you don't mind, I won't sit down. I feel too restless and excited." She stared about her now, for the first time, drinking in the room with the sudden greedy gaze of youth. "This is a lovely room, isn't it? Is this the famous Green Room everybody talks about?"

"Yes," said Pauline. "And they've kept it more or less as it used to be."

"It is a pity we don't have Green Rooms now." Ann went on staring. "This is a terribly exciting place," she added, with a childlike confidential air.

"A lot of people find it rather frightening—spooky," said Pauline.

"I'm sure it's absolutely crammed with ghosts, just longing to show themselves and whisper in your ear——"

"Hoy, stop it!" cried Pauline.

"No," said Ann, "but the point is—they aren't the usual kind of ghosts—murderers or mad old women—they'd just be actors and actresses, our sort of people, excited about the Theatre just like us. I don't think I'd mind them at all. And I'm sure they're here, dozens of them. Miss Fraser," she continued, in an excited whisper, "why don't you sit up here late at night—and watch——"

What it was to be twenty-three! "My God, no," cried Pauline. "I'd be terrified." And suddenly, with a chill bristle of fear, she knew she *would* be

28

terrified, was in fact rather frightened at that very moment. She sat down, and let the girl prowl round the room, looking at the portraits, by herself.

"I suppose these people must have played here, when it was grander than it is now," said Ann over her shoulder. "Edmund Kean—he *looks* a good actor somehow, doesn't he? Helen Faucit—rather sweet. The Elder Matthews—obviously a terrific comic, in spite of the Elder business." She moved on. "Mrs. Yates—I like it when they call them *Missis*, don't you? *Watercolour Sketch of Miss Jenny Villiers in the part of Viola, Presented by the Barton Spa Shakespearean Society.* Jenny Villiers. Nice name. I've never heard of her before, yet somehow it sounds familiar. And I'll bet *she* had to pester people too before she could get a chance, even though she does look so sweet and sad, and wear ringlets. Hello, what was that?"

Pauline stared at her, startled by her tone. "Why—it wasn't anything, was it? I mean—I didn't see anything."

They stared at each other for a moment. Ann sounded breathless but spoke very quietly. "No—but—did you feel something?"

"No, not really," said Pauline, confused now. "I think it was you who startled me."

"I'm sorry," said Ann slowly and carefully.

"But you see, just when I'd said that—you know, about Jenny Villiers—I seemed to feel a sudden little rush of air—very cold air—and then some-body—or something—seemed to whisk past me. Oh!" And she stared at the floor.

Pauline jumped up, every nerve jangling. "What? What is it?"

Ann pointed. Lying on the floor, several feet from the nearer glass case, was an old-fashioned gauntlet glove, olive green and red. She picked it up. "It wasn't there before, you know, Miss Fraser. I'll swear it wasn't. I couldn't possibly have missed it."

"Part of an old costume," said Pauline, going nearer to inspect it. "They have some bits of old costumes and props in there." She indicated the glass case. "It must have fallen out. That's it. And that's what you must have felt."

"I suppose so," said Ann slowly. "Only it couldn't have fallen out. It must have jumped out, to have brushed past me like that. Oh!" And she stared again.

"I wish you wouldn't do that," cried Pauline, robbed of her assumed calm. "What is it this time?"

"The door of that case," replied Ann apologetic-ally. "You see, it isn't open. How could the glove——"

"The door must have suddenly sprung open," said Pauline hastily, "and then swung to again. They often do."

"Yes, I suppose so." She was staring at Pauline now. "But it's a bit peculiar, you know—a glove behaving like that."

"No, it isn't, and for goodness sake, child, don't start pretending anything queer has happened. I have to be around here for the next ten days—and you haven't. Just put it back."

Ann went to the glass case. "I think *she* did it," she murmured. "Jenny What's-her-name."

"Nonsense! Now let's be sensible." And Pauline walked up to the door on the stage side. "Mr. Cheveril will be back any minute." She opened the door so that anybody coming up the stairs from the stage could be heard. "I know he won't want to see you. I'll have to try and persuade him. You'd better wait outside."

"But if I was still here, he'd *have* to talk to me."

"No, he wouldn't," said Pauline, rather crossly. This was a nice child, probably clever too, but she could be trying. "Don't forget people are always wanting to see him, and he hates it, particularly just now. Your only chance is to do what I tell you."

Ann gave in at once. "Yes, of course. And don't think I'm not grateful."

31

Pauline was still near the open door, with an ear alert for any footfalls below. "I think he may be coming up now. You'd better get behind that door there, and wait. I'll do my best for you."

"I think," said Ann, making for the door, "you're a darling."

As soon as the girl was out of the room, Pauline went down to the glass case, where the gauntlet glove reposed innocently, and stared at it speculatively for a few moments. She tried the little catch that opened the case, and it seemed secure enough. Finally, she took out the glove and had a good look at it, as if it might be part of a conjuring trick. Then, hearing Cheveril come into the room, she hastily restored the glove, leaving the case still open.

Cheveril was carrying a number of letters as well as the script of his play. "I went along to the stage door. Two letters for you," he said, handing them over, "and all these for me, mostly rubbish. That scene's all right now. We've made a neat little cut. They'll be wanting you in a minute or two, Pauline." There was a little writing desk in the alcove on the stage side of the room, and now Cheveril took his letters there.

Pauline lingered. "I was just going down. Martin, there's a girl here. She's with a local repertory company—and she's taken the day off and come here just to see you."

32

Cheveril moved his shoulders impatiently as he sat down. "Otley shouldn't have let her in." He opened a letter and glanced at it. He cared nothing about the girl but knew he was behaving rather badly to Pauline, giving her nothing but his back. But even those few minutes work on the stage had left him exhausted, and he was anxious for Pauline to go and leave him alone.

"Otley tried to stop her, but he couldn't," she explained. "She's a determined young woman— and I shouldn't be surprised if she's quite a good little actress. Now she's here, you'll see her—won't you?"

Without turning, he told her, firmly, No.

"Now don't be mean, Martin——"

He looked over his shoulder this time. "She'd no right to push herself in. And there's nothing I can do for her except to tell her that I don't care for her manners. No, I'm sorry, Pauline. But if she were a young Duse or Bernhardt, I still wouldn't care. I'm just not interested any more. I haven't to find any more promising young actresses—thank God! And I don't see why I should be victimised in this way."

Pauline was reproachful. "Martin, this is all wrong. I hate it."

Somebody called up the stairs: "Miss Fraser, you're wanted on the stage."

33

From the doorway Pauline cried: "I wish something would happen to you, Martin. I don't know what, but something so big and strange that you couldn't explain it away—just *feel* it." And then she banged the door behind her.

While Cheveril looked through the rest of his letters, he heard the other door open, but did not turn round. Then a young voice, needlessly explaining itself: "I'm the young actress, Mr. Cheveril. My name's Ann Seward."

He did not even look at her. "You'd no right to come in here. Will you please go?"

"I've acted in lots of your plays—and loved them."

Cheveril hastily tore up two envelopes and a letter from a woman offering him the vast idiotic scenario for a play about reincarnation. "Yes, but I'm busy—and I don't want to see you."

The girl was incredulous. "Not even just to *look* at me?"

"No," he replied angrily, without turning. "Will you please go at once?"

There was a pause, a strange little pause. "You'll be sorry soon you said that." She spoke with an odd certainty. A rum youngster, with rather a good voice, but he did not propose to recognise her existence. He could hear her moving about the room, and wondered what she was up to. Then

34

she said, to his astonishment: "Look—the glove's
on the floor again. Even the ghosts are on my side.
Be careful."

He did not move until several moments after he
had heard the door close behind her. When he did
move, he discovered that she had taken a gauntlet
glove from one of the cases, which was open, and
had thrown it on the floor, as if hurling a challenge.
Some long-dead and forgotten Rosalind had worn
this glove, and he examined it, and smoothed it out
with a melancholy tenderness. When this glove had
first been worn, bright in its green and scarlet,
down on that stage, the Forest of Arden, where
they fleeted the time carelessly as they did in the
golden world, had not seemed so far away, so
irrecoverably lost in time, as it did now to him, a
dry weary man in a half-ruined world. There was,
in this absurd glove, which had something
essentially feminine about it, more than a hint of
that Theatre which had once enchanted him and
now seemed a barren playground. He had meant
to put it back where it belonged but found that he
had carried it to the desk, and so he let it lie there
while he finished off his letters, writing a brief note
to a friend, a weary longish letter to his agent, and
leaving or destroying the rest. Now and again the
glove caught his eye, and there seemed a touch of
mockery about its green and scarlet bravery.

35

4

CHEVERIL heard the door open again, and this time he swept round, ready to demolish the wretched girl. But it was Otley. "Dr. Cave's here, Mr. Cheveril."

"Good! Send him in." Cheveril left the desk. "And—I say—if you've a drop of drink left from that party, you might ask the doctor what he'd like."

Otley grinned. "Certainly. He mightn't object to a whisky-and-soda. What about you, Mr. Cheveril?"

36

"Not for me, thanks. But I may need a glass of water—if you don't mind."

Dr. Cave, one of the large hearty kind, made a brisk entrance. "Well, I thought I'd better look in and have a word with you before letting you have this stuff." And he produced a small bottle of white tablets, with that air of triumph so many doctors assume at these moments, as if they had just conjured the magic stuff out of the air.

"I'm much obliged. Sit down, doctor, and smoke a cigarette with me—and have a drink."

Dr. Cave patted his knees, and smiled. "Well, I told Otley I might just risk a small whisky-and-soda." He accepted and lit a cigarette. "I want you to stay in that nice big armchair if you can, for an hour or two."

Otley arrived with the whisky-and-soda and a glass of water. "There you are, gentlemen. And I'll see you're not disturbed."

"Thanks," said Cheveril. "But I'd like to see you for a moment after the doctor's gone."

"And that'll be very soon," Dr. Cave told them both. "I'm a busy man." He waited until Otley went out, and then held up his glass. "Here's luck to the play! Um—better whisky than I can get, when I can get it. You theatrical people know where to find it. Good little chap Otley, isn't he? Sometimes see him at a little club we have here.

We think he's made a good job out of running this old theatre of ours. What do you say?"

Cheveril said that he thought so too. Then he leaned back and closed his eyes for a moment, suddenly feeling empty and exhausted; and this turned his visitor back at once into a physician.

"Well, Mr. Cheveril," he began, in his professional manner, "I'm taking your word for it that it's impossible for you to rest properly during these next few days. You've got a very low blood pressure. I won't say it's dangerously low—I don't know enough about you to say that—but it's low enough to explain why you feel exhausted and depressed. Mind you, there may be other factors——"

"What other factors?"

"Nervous or mental. Loss of energy is a curious business. But I'm no psychologist," the doctor continued hastily. "What I do know is that by driving yourself you're taking the risk of having a serious breakdown. You're not a young man, and mustn't pretend to yourself you are."

"I don't," said Cheveril, quite truthfully. He made a little impatient movement.

Dr. Cave showed him the tablets. "Now these things are new, as I told you this morning. I don't pretend to know a lot about them. But I suggest you take two now, and settle down quietly in that chair for an hour or so, relax and don't bother about anything—and then they ought to see you comfortably through your rehearsing to-night. Then try two more in the morning."

"All right," said Cheveril, taking out two of the tablets.

"That's it. Just take them with a sip of water—they'll soon dissolve inside you." He sipped his whisky. "And don't you worry if you feel a bit queer in about half-an-hour or so. Keep quiet—and rest—that's all."

After Cheveril had swallowed the tablets, he stared thoughtfully at the doctor and then said: "Tell me. I suppose you see a good deal of suffering, don't you?"

"Yes. Seen a few pretty bad specimens since I saw you last. Why?"

"I've just been arguing with one of my actresses, an old friend of mine. She was accusing me of being bored and cynical and bitter. And she wouldn't have it that that was because I saw that life was so hard and unpleasant for other people. She said it was because I'd had too much success and had had it too easy—nothing to struggle for—and so on——"

"She might be right," said Dr. Cave. "But where do I come in?"

Cheveril was frank with him. "I was thinking

39

that you're a better argument for her case than for mine. Nothing bored and cynical and bitter about you."

"Certainly not. But that's different. When I see people suffer, it's my job to try to pull them out of it. I'm fighting for life. That keeps me going."

"Perhaps I ought to be fighting for life," said Cheveril.

"Everybody ought to be." Dr. Cave stood up.

"If they think it's worth fighting for."

"Of course it is. Your trouble is—and here you're worse off than I am—that your job as a writer depends on your imagination, which probably magnifies other people's troubles and all the misery in the world. Especially—and this is the point to remember—when your blood pressure's down and everything seems an effort and you feel depressed." He picked up his bag and hat.

"You're probably right," Cheveril sighed. "Though the fact that I'm really just a bunch of arteries and blood-pumping apparatus doesn't fill me with sudden joy."

"There you go," cried Dr. Cave briskly. "Exaggerating again. I didn't say you were only that, but I do say it plays its part. So just be careful. Remember what I said. And better give me a ring in the morning. Now—stay there, make yourself comfortable—and try to relax." He made for the door just as Otley looked in. "Otley, see that Mr. Cheveril isn't disturbed for an hour or so. He must be quiet for a time. And switch a few of these lights off. No, I can find my way out. And thanks for the drink. 'Bye!"

It was surprising how the Green Room changed as soon as Otley had switched off most of the lights. All that were left were a small lamp on the desk behind Cheveril and a wall bracket, of three amber shaded lights, not far from his armchair. The place looked twice the size. Otley, lingering near the door, was lost in shadow. "You said you wanted to see me when the doctor had gone."

"Yes. Come and sit down for a minute or two."

Otley perched his tubby little self on the chair that Dr. Cave had used, very near Cheveril. "They think a lot of Dr. Cave round here," he remarked, "though I've never been to him myself, being one of the healthy ones. Given you something to take, hasn't he, Mr. Cheveril?"

"Yes, these tablets," said Cheveril drowsily. He shook out two of them on to the palm of his hand as he talked. "By the way, there'll probably be a call from London coming through for me in about half-an-hour, from Sir George Gavin, and as it's important you'd better put it through to me here, please. No other calls. And if you can manage it, don't let anybody come in. I'm

41

supposed to rest before to-night's rehearsal."

Otley looked hard at him. "Right you are, Mr. Cheveril. I'll be just along there in my office. Better take those tablets, hadn't you?"

There was something vaguely wrong about this, but Cheveril couldn't bother to work out what it was. "Yes, I suppose so."

It was Otley who handed him the glass of water, so that he could swallow the tablets, and after he had done this and handed the glass back to Otley, the latter noticed the gauntlet glove on the desk. "Hello, how did you get here?"

"What's that?"

Otley showed him the glove.

"Oh—I found it lying on the floor. What's the matter?"

Otley sat down again, still holding the glove. "They used to tell funny stories about one or two of the things here," he said softly. "Including this glove. You know the sort of stuff—just super-stition."

"Well, I'm not superstitious." Cheveril yawned. He did not feel sleepy in the ordinary way but rather felt that at any moment he might slowly float out of that chair.

Otley's reply was too hearty. "Neither am I, Mr. Cheveril. Not a bit. But of course with an old place like this—you know—you do get funny ideas sometimes. I'd better put this back where it belongs, in the case over there."

"Who was supposed to wear it?" Cheveril enquired idly.

"Nobody really famous. But she made a bit of a stir here about a hundred years ago and was a great local favourite—and then went and died young. You've probably never heard of her. Jenny Villiers."

Cheveril stared at him. "Jenny Villiers," he repeated slowly. "That's odd. Very odd."

"Why, Mr. Cheveril?"

"I was thinking about her, the other night," said Cheveril, still speaking slowly. "I'll tell you how it happened. I'd been looking somebody up in *Who's Who In The Theatre*, and then I went on idly turning the pages and came to that section near the end called the *Theatrical and Musical Obituary*."

Otley knew it. "Gives the date of everybody's death and how old they were when they died."

"It does." He continued dreamily: "And that repetition of the word *died* after every name gives it all a curiously melancholy ring . . ."

There was a pause. Otley had to prompt him. "And you happened to notice this girl's name——?"

Cheveril nodded. "*Jenny Villiers, Actress, died Fifteenth of November* 1846, *aged* 24. You see. I remember even those details. The fact is, I began

43   D

wondering about her." He said no more for a moment or two, then went on slowly, rather heavily: "She must have had some success, young as she was, to be included in that list. Yet she was only twenty-four when she died. Everything coming right for her . . . success at last . . . and then she's snuffed out like a candle . . ." He stopped again, and looked at Otley with a sleepy apologetic smile. "Jenny Villiers. The name was charming. Probably assumed."

"I expect so," said Otley. "Bit too good to be true, you might say."

"The Jenny half of it," Cheveril continued, in the slow dreamy fashion so unlike his usual manner, "so young and feminine, bright, almost impudent. . . . The Villiers half so grand, aristocratic, rather bogus in the old theatrical style. . . . I tried to imagine the girl, in the little time she had, smiling and curtseying in the light of the oil-lamp floats and gas battens of that queer, remote, stuffy old Theatre of the 'Forties. . . . I was fascinated . . . queerly moved too . . . as if . . ."

"As if what, Mr. Cheveril?" Otley enquired.

Cheveril managed a suggestion of a laugh. "No, don't let us be fantastic. But I wondered about her, almost began to see her. And then I had to stop. Something happened. Yes, somebody rang me up——" He stopped, as if he felt the touch of

44

icy finger. He stared at Otley as if the man were a ghost. "Why, it was you."

"Well, I did ring you up one night, Mr. Cheveril," said Otley. "About you trying your new play here. Was that the time?"

"That was the time. It was then I agreed to come here."

"Bit of a coincidence," cried Otley, well out of reach of any icy fingers, "when you come to look at it. You thinking about her, and then, without knowing it, agreeing to come to the very theatre she last acted in—eh?"

Cheveril had recovered. He observed, with mock solemnity: "If our lives followed mysterious hidden patterns, designs from behind the veil, then here is a good example——"

Otley did not know how to take this. "Well, yes," he said uncertainly.

"And our lives don't, you see. But that's why I said it was odd—very odd."

Otley smiled, nodded, and then got out of his chair. "I'll put this souvenir back where it came from." He went trotting across to the glass case. "And if you'd like to know a bit more about Jenny Villiers, there's one or two things here might interest you."

"No," Cheveril called sharply. "It doesn't matter."

45

His tone puzzled Otley, as indeed it puzzled himself, for he had no idea why he had spoken like that. "Oh well, of course not, Mr. Cheveril, if you want to rest. No reason why you should bother——"

"No, no, I'm sorry. I don't know why I said that. This stuff I've taken, probably. I'd be glad to have a look at anything you've got there."

"There's a little book about her," said Otley, busy with the glass case, "just a sort of tribute some local chap wrote at the time. And then there's this little watercolour sketch of her as Viola—you might not have noticed it." And he came back with them.

"Thanks," said Cheveril, taking the sketch and then staring at it. "Um. So this was poor little Jenny Villiers."

"Your hand's shaking, Mr. Cheveril. Sure you're all right?"

"Yes, it's only that stuff. The doctor said I might feel rather queer. Kind of floating feeling." He looked at the booklet now, and read out the title page: "*Jenny Villiers, A Tribute and a Memoir— by Augustus Ponsonby Esquire, Honorary Secretary of the Barton Spa Shakespearean Society*. . . . A page of quotations first, culled from the Bard, of course—

> *Be absolute for death; either death or life*
> *Shall thereby be the sweeter* . . .

46

Be absolute for death? A strange idea, that, Otley. What's next?

> *When to the session of sweet silent thought*
> *I summon up remembrance of things past.* . . .

An obvious choice. But this isn't. Listen—

> *Make me a willow cabin at your gate,*
> *And call upon my soul within the house* . . ."

"I seem to remember that," said Otley, who had sat himself down again. "*Twelfth Night*—Viola—isn't it?"

"It is," said Cheveril, rather absently.

"Well, you see, I think that was the part they liked her best in. But I doubt if you'll find that little book worth reading, Mr. Cheveril. Old-fashioned pompous stuff. Her story was simple enough. They had a stock company here in those days, under an actor-manager called Edmund Ludlow. Jenny Villiers came here from the Norfolk Circuit, and got some leading parts. She fell in love with the leading juvenile, Julian Napier, but he suddenly left the company for a London engagement. Then she was taken ill—and died. And Napier didn't last much longer. He went to New York, started drinking hard, and soon finished himself. That's all there is to it, really."

"Nothing in it," said Cheveril slowly. "Every-

47

thing in it." He waited for a moment, and then murmured, more to himself than to his companion:

> *"Be absolute for death; either death or life*
> *Shall thereby be the sweeter . . ."*

Otley was preparing to leave him. "And I shan't forget what you said, Mr. Cheveril—you'll just take that one call from London."

"Yes, please," said Cheveril drowsily. And then, as Otley withdrew, Cheveril found himself muttering: *"And call upon my soul within the house . . ."* It was as if he had never known the line before, as if it came from some strange masterpiece. *And call upon my soul within the house. . . .* As if there were some other Shakespeare nobody ever mentioned, whose tragedies were comedies, whose comedies were tragedies, played triumphantly somewhere in a lost kingdom. . . .

It was very quiet. Even the little singing noise in his ears, which he had known ever since the doctors had told him his blood pressure was too low, was quieter now. The old brown dusk, which had enveloped him when he was outside the door listening to his own party, had seeped through into this Green Room. The alcoves were in deeper shadow. The place no longer had any shape and size. How many tablets had he taken? Two? Or

had he taken two again and stupidly made it four?
He made an effort and pushed himself deeper into
the chair, but then felt that the chair was floating
too. Well, he could float into sleep. Time was
losing its cutting edge, as it always did in that
twilit region between waking and sleeping. Yet
there was in him somewhere one remaining spark
of alertness, one solitary sentry still awake above
the vast drowsy castle of his mind. What next
then? Who goes there? . . .

5

THERE was a faint ray of light, thinner than a moonbeam coming through cloud and dusty glass, that had not been in the room before. It did not come from anywhere: it was simply there. As Cheveril stared at it, he gradually became aware of a figure in black that moved in this light. Then, half-way across the room, in its progress towards the door that led to the stage, the figure stopped. Cheveril could see now that it was a youngish man, one of those grotesquely thin creatures in Early Victorian costume that Cruikshank and *Phiz* were

50

always drawing. Cheveril had time to tell himself that that was probably all it was, the memory of some Dickens illustration projected into the darkness. But then, the man turned and looked at him, with despairing eyes in a hollow white face. And Cheveril felt deathly cold and afraid. This was no conjuring trick with the memory of an old illustration. This came from no book. The man stared at him, almost accusingly, out of some chill graveyard sort of life. Cheveril tried to speak but found it impossible to make the simplest sound. Then the figure glided away, towards the far door, and the thin glimmer of light faded; and then the Green Room was just as it was before, brown dusk and silence.

But was it? Cheveril stared harder. The room itself was the same, no doubt, but somehow there were differences. Where was the tall glass case in the alcove at the other side of the room? And the walls were not quite the same; something there, perhaps the portraits and old theatre bills, had been changed. Cheveril's eyes pricked and ached. He closed them, and allowed himself to float a little in comfort. And it was then that he heard voices, quite clearly, as clearly as he had heard Otley's and the doctor's a few minutes before. But these voices were singing, first a man and then two or three girls; and after a moment or two he recognised what it was they were singing, the rollicking old *Villikins and His Dinah*. The refrain came nearer, and then he opened his eyes. Beyond the pool of sensible light in which he sat there was, as before, a ring of shadow, but now beyond that ring, illuminating most of the room, was a soft golden light, which like the faint glimmer he had seen before did not appear to come from anywhere in particular, but which, like the light in a dream, was simply there. Nothing unreal about it—there it was, plain to be seen—but nevertheless he knew at once that it was not existing in the same dimensions as the light above his chair, which now appeared to be slowly fading.

A voice outside, a deep ripe theatrical voice, was calling: "What's happening, Sam me boy?"

Some other man, again an actor, replied: "Mr. Ludlow wants to see everybody in the Green Room."

The first voice, much nearer now, cried: "Ay, ay—so shall it be. Come, ladies, the Green Room."

And then in they came, seven or eight of them, the girls pushing and chattering and giggling, all in the costumes of Eighteen-Forties. One young man was solemnly smoking a large curved pipe. The owner of the deep ripe voice, an old actor not unlike Alfred Leathers, was called John Stokes. The last to enter, an oldish commanding woman who was carrying a generous shopping basket, was addressed as Mrs. Ludlow.

By the time these people were occupying the upper half of the room, Cheveril's own corner of it appeared to be almost in darkness. In his astonishment at the appearance of these solid apparitions, he had involuntarily risen from his chair, and after standing and staring for a moment or two, he had moved a few paces forward. There was nothing thin and spectral about the scene before him. It was all solidly there, down to the smallest wrinkles on the face of the old actor, Stokes, and the faint stains on some of the shawls and dresses of the women. The smoke from the young actor's pipe went curling and wreathing, as plain as the smoke from the doctor's cigarette. But the young actor and the rest, Cheveril felt at once, were not there in the sense that the doctor and Otley and Pauline had been there. They were there, he knew, to be seen and heard but not to be lived with. It was like staring close at hand into something between a film and a scene in a play. He knew there was no possible communication between him and these people—or appearances. And though it was odd and wonderful, there was nothing challenging and frightening about it, as there had been, in one cold flash, when the eyes in that hollow white face had stared into his.

53

"Did you find anything nice, Mrs. Ludlow?" one of the younger actresses was asking. She had a snub nose and rather greasy auburn ringlets.

"Yes, my dear," said Mrs. Ludlow, in a deep solemn tone. She was evidently in the Siddons tradition. "Four pork chops and a fine cauliflower. Mr. Ludlow is extremely fond of pork chops— fortunately. He will need all his strength to sustain him through this crisis."

"Oh—dear!" cried another girl, a little dark one. "Has something terrible happened?"

"Mr. Ludlow," said his wife, "will explain."

There was now a tremendous clatter from outside, with cries of "Gee up!" and "Steady, my steed," and a little fat man, with comedian stamped all over him, made a big entrance, riding a large umbrella. He pulled up sharply, then swept off his dingy high hat. "Ladies, your servant," he cried, and then went elaborately through the pantomime business of dismounting and handing the umbrella, as horse, to old John Stokes, who at once entered into the spirit of the performance. "Give me 'orse a rub-down, fellow, an' mouthful o' hay."

"Ay, ay, sir," cried Stokes, as groom. "Will your honour be staying here the night?"

"S'death!" roared the comic. "I am on urgent business for the Dook."

"Sam Moon!" cried Mrs. Ludlow reproachfully.

"Ma'am?"

"Save your drollery for to-night's performance, when you will need it. At the moment it is out of place."

"Sorry to 'ear it, ma'am," said Moon, screwing up his comical round face, "most sorry to 'ear it. But still we've 'ad troubles before—an' said Good-bye to 'em. A-ha, 'ere comes our Mr. Napier."

Mr. Napier, who had come striding in at that moment, was obviously the juvenile lead, and a handsome haughty young man with long black hair, the complete romantic of the 'Forties. He wore a dark blue stock, a tight-fitting lighter blue coat, and light grey strapped trousers. For a moment or two Cheveril stared at him as if he were no more than a pretty waxwork figure, but then, as if a tiny Otley were perched in his ear whispering, there returned to him what Otley had said about Jenny Villiers—*She fell in love with the leading juvenile, Julian Napier.* . . . And this was Julian Napier. A cold excitement took possession of Cheveril, and for a while the scene before him was blurred and so much of the colour was drained out of it that it looked like a huge daguerreotype. The voices were farther away too, but he heard them easily enough.

"I hope this won't take long," Julian Napier was saying, in his haughty leading-gentleman style. "I have an engagement with two gentlemen at the *White Hart* in half-an-hour. What's the matter now, Mrs. Ludlow?"

She was stiff with him, clearly no favourite of hers. "Mr. Ludlow will explain, Mr. Napier. And you may be sure that Mr. Ludlow would not call the company together at this hour unless it were something serious."

"Possibly not," said Napier. "But I must keep my engagement at the *White Hart*."

"Are they swells, Julian me boy?" asked Moon.

"One of them's a baronet," said Napier. "He took a box, the other night." He glanced round the company. "Miss Vincent not here?"

"I don't see her," replied Mrs. Ludlow, grimly.

There were some exclamations of surprise and exchanges of glances among the company.

"Look here," Napier demanded, "what's happened?"

"All in good time."

The actress with the snub nose and auburn ringlets said that she thought she saw Miss Vincent with Mr. Ludlow just before the company came up there.

"Then you were mistaken," Mrs. Ludlow told her majestically.

"Who was it then?" asked the little dark actress. "I didn't think it was Miss Vincent."

But now Mr. Ludlow himself strode in. (*They had a stock company here in those days*, Otley had said, *under an actor-manager called Edmund Ludlow*. But where was Jenny Villiers? And surely the scene was losing colour and definition again?) Mr. Ludlow was a square oldish man, with an immense chest and a Roman nose, very much a presence. "Ladies and gentlemen," he announced, giving enormous value to each vowel, "Miss Vincent has left us." There were cries of astonishment and annoyance, at which Mr. Ludlow smiled grimly, like Coriolanus. "Left us in circumstances of basest treachery——"

"And still owing much money in the town," said Mrs. Ludlow. "Over five pounds at Trimbleby's alone."

"So I believe, my love," said Mr. Ludlow, in his milder and domestic voice. Then terrible, Coriolanus, again: "I will not speak of ingratitude——"

"I will," cried Mrs. Ludlow. "The ungrateful creature!"

"But, as you know," Mr. Ludlow reminded the company, "I proposed to revive *The Maniac of the Wreck* chiefly because of Miss Vincent, and although she knew this, and allowed herself to be

57

billed in the leading role, I have evidence now that she had already agreed to accept the offer from Mr. Buckstone—for small parts——"

"*Very* small parts," his wife added, with some relish.

"At least a week ago. Inexcusable of course. Black treachery. In the old days she would have found it impossible to live down such an act, but now, when ambition is preferred to honour, when money and false pride reign undisputed——"

It was Julian Napier, impatient, who interrupted him. "Well, the point is, she's gone. And we certainly can't do *The Maniac of the Wreck* without her. And what about our *Twelfth Night*—also widely announced? We haven't a Viola now."

Mr. Ludlow frowned heavily upon him. "If you will kindly allow me, Mr. Napier, to discuss my business. Clearly we can't do *The Maniac*, so I'm proposing to put back *The Soldier's Widow, Or The Deserted Mill*, which always takes." But the company took it with a groan.

"It depends, as I've said before," the old actor Stokes remarked, "on your broadsword com-bat——"

"Yes, yes, I agree," Ludlow told him. "We'll have special rehearsals this time of the broadsword combat. And as for our *Twelfth Night*, we can put it off for a week or so——"

58

"While you try to find a Viola worth seeing?" cried Napier contemptuously. "Not much chance."

Mr. Ludlow, who had obviously built up the scene for this moment, was now solemnly triumphant. "I *have* a Viola worth seeing. And unless I am much mistaken, a far better one than Miss Vincent's. A Lady Teazle and a Rosalind and an Ophelia too." He held up a hand to check the tumult. "Mr. Kettle remembered that our friend Mr. Murphy of the Norfolk Circuit recommended us a good juvenile female lead who wanted a change. Mr. Kettle saw her and has brought her back with him. She has already given me some excellent readings from classic roles." He turned to the door on the stage side, and called: "Walter, you can do the honours."

The scene immediately steadied itself, sharpened its definition, and the colour came flooding back into every gown and shawl, every ringlet and eye. There entered now that same thin, grotesque-looking fellow who had paused, in the faint ghostly light, to stare at Cheveril. His tight frock-coat and pantaloons had once been black but were now shiny and greenish with age and hard wear. Everything about him was shabby and defeated except his burning eyes. But now he was smiling, radiant with the brief happiness of the tragic and doomed kind of men. He was no longer aware of

59 E

Cheveril (if, that is, he had been before): but Cheveril found himself terribly aware of him.

"Ladies and gentlemen," said Walter Kettle, with a hint of parody of Ludlow's grand manner, "may I present to you our new juvenile female lead—Miss Jenny Villiers——"

She floated in, a stir of new light about her, a rather tall, slender girl, wearing a little bodice and a wide dress of flowered muslin, and, instead of the bonnet worn by all the other women, a flat-crowned straw hat with a wide curved brim that revealed her fair ringlets and her rather long delicate face. She was ablaze with happy excitement. And there was in him somewhere, Cheveril felt, a pulse that quickened its beat to keep time with her heart.

Smilingly she curtsied, and smilingly the others applauded. And then she dropped a small gaily-coloured purse. Kettle tried to pick it up, but Julian Napier was too quick for him, and was offering it to her while Kettle scowled at him. Jenny Villiers lifted her eyes to Napier's handsome height, and then smiled at him.

"Yours, I think, Miss Villiers."

"Thank you."

"I'm your new leading juvenile—Julian Napier."

And as the two stood looking at each other, the whole scene was for a moment completely silent,

60

frozen; and then the light began to fade slowly, and all the sharp edges vanished, and the colour became muddy and dim, and the brown dusk rose like a swift silent tide. There was no longer a sound. But Cheveril, who had not moved, felt that the thick curtain of a hundred years had not yet descended, and fancied that he still saw vague shapes in motion, curtseying or bowing, as if Jenny, now a mere patch of greyness in the gloom, were being introduced to the company; but very soon even this thin spectral movement shredded to mere tatters of darkness and vanished; and then there was nothing, nothing but a sense of bewilderment, of loss, and heartache . . .

6

HE was back in his armchair, with the lights
above him burning steadily and sensibly, and all
was as it was when Otley left him there. "So
that's how it began," he found himself muttering,
"and of course that's how it would begin." But
was it all beginning again now? Had it happened
like that—or was it still happening—or had he
been dreaming? But of course he had been
dreaming. Out of the mysterious deep ocean of
our secret life one wave, this strangely vivid
dream, had risen, to wash over him, leaving him

62

shivering with a sense of loss, of vague heartache, desolate still but not so utterly weary and dry, like a skeleton in a desert, as he had felt before. The tablets, of course. They were probably now hard at work inside him, performing their little miracles of chemistry, to pump the blood more vigorously through his arteries. And his dreaming unconscious self, knowing no science, had had to create the image of a tall slender girl with silken ringlets and then dazzle him with her. And so out of that glass case and his talk with Otley, out of a glove and a booklet and watercolour sketch, had popped poor little Jenny Villiers, dead and forgotten, everywhere but here, these hundred years. The dream of course had arisen from the sense of loss, whatever that might amount to, and not the sense of loss from the dream. However, it had been a good dream, uncommonly vivid and lifelike. Some of its incidents and odd scraps of its talk now returned to him. Strange what the dreaming self could achieve, effortlessly in the dark! If he had been commanded to write a scene like that, against the background of a provincial theatre of the Eighteen-Forties, he would never, he felt, have contrived without research to have created it with so many convincing details. Well, he owed something to Barton Spa's pious regard for its old theatre and Green Room, and to the tall

glass case over there. He gave it a grateful glance—
only to find that it wasn't there.

And then a voice said, quite distinctly: "Yes,
dear, but you can make more of it than that."
And he knew that voice at once; it belonged to
Mrs. Ludlow.

"It's a big scene," she continued, "and properly
done it always takes famously."

The strange cone of light was smaller this time
but rather brighter than it had been before.
Jenny Villiers was no longer wearing a hat and her
pretty muslin but was in a plain dark-brown
working dress. Mrs. Ludlow was still bonneted and
shawled, a majestic figure. He knew at once that
they were rehearsing here in the Green Room.
There was nothing ghostly about them; they were
both solidly there; but so too, expressed in some
inexplicable fashion, was the gap in time: they
were here but they were also a hundred years
away.

"Now when I did it," Mrs. Ludlow was saying,
"I always got on tiptoe and stretched my hands out
on *Horror, horror*, and then on *Distraction, Come!* I
crossed my hands in front of my face. I'll show
you what I mean, dear—just watch me."

Cheveril knew immediately, even before he
caught the twinkle in Jenny's eye, that the girl felt
that this stuff was false and stagey. Standing on

tiptoe with her arms outstretched and looking
rather like a vast mad crow, Mrs. Ludlow in her
deepest contralto cried "Oh, horror, horror!"
Continuing then in her ordinary tone, she said:
"Then—so and so and so and so—slowly coming
down, you see, dear, till you get to 'Distraction,
come possess me now for I will be *thy* bride'—like
this——" And she bowed her head, shuddering,
and crossed hands before her face. At which Jenny
suddenly giggled.

"What's the matter, dear?"

"I'm sorry, Mrs. Ludlow. I do see what you
mean, and you're doing it so beautifully. It's just
that—well, this Moorish princess sounds such an
idiot, asking to be Distraction's bride."

"Properly played, Miss Villiers," said Mrs.
Ludlow in a tone of dignified rebuke, "I assure
you the part never fails. Ask Mr. Ludlow." She
turned, speaking into what was still darkness to
Cheveril. "Yes, Walter? Am I wanted on the
stage? Very well. I'm just taking Miss Villiers
through the big scene in the *Moorish Princess*—
which she doesn't seem quite to appreciate.
Here's the book—just see what you can do."

Her place in the cone of light was taken by
Kettle, who looked more than ever like some
grotesque out of an Early Victorian illustration.
Nevertheless, Cheveril felt strongly that he was a

65

living suffering man, probably underpaid and
overworked as Ludlow's stage-manager. There
was something about him oddly sympathetic to
Cheveril.

"Oh dear," Jenny was saying, "I hope I haven't
offended her. You see, I couldn't help laughing,
not at her but at the part—it's so silly. You must
admit it is. Listen."

She assumed a tragic posture and then, speaking
in a false tragic tone, went through the movements
that Mrs. Ludlow had just shown her:

"O Carlos! noble youth! How have my fears
Betray'd thee to thy doom!
Inhuman father! Noble, injured youth!
Methinks I see thee stretch'd upon the rack,
Hear thy expiring moans. O horror, horror!
Naught I can do can save him—Vain, alas!
Vain are my maiden tears and pray'rs.
Distraction, come possess me now, for I
Will be *thy* bride."

But now she looked earnestly at Kettle. "You
see, Mr. Kettle. I can't act it because I can't
believe in it. No girl ever behaved like that, or
talked like that. It isn't *true*."

"Of course it isn't," Kettle told her. "But then
no girl ever talked like Viola or Rosalind."

"But that's not the same thing. We'd like to talk

66

as Viola and Rosalind do. It's what we *feel*, turned into wonderful words. But this isn't. It's all just silly stuff. Asking for Distraction as if it were some old admirer who lived round the corner. Now—isn't it silly?"

Kettle replied in a humorous whisper: "Yes. I've thought so for years. Language, situations, gestures—all ridiculous. You're quite right."

"Oh—bless you for saying that!" she cried. "You see, if she only said something quite simple and direct—like—'O Carlos—noble Carlos—because I was frightened I have betrayed you—perhaps to your death.' Just standing there, quite still, looking down on him——"

"Do it like that."

"Oh—do you think I dare?"

As they stood there, looking at each other, Cheveril found himself standing only just outside the sharp edge of light, found himself talking to them across the invisible gulf of years: "Yes, my dears—yes. Dare—break through the routine, smash the old worn moulds. Dare, as we all must do, to give it new life——"

"All right," she told Kettle, her face alight, "I will."

A voice, very remote to Cheveril, came through the dark to say that Miss Villiers and Mr. Kettle were wanted on the stage.

67

"Coming," Kettle called, and moved out of the light at once, to vanish. Jenny followed him rather reluctantly, the light moving with her but rapidly fading too.

"Jenny!" And Cheveril was astonished to discover that it was his voice now that was calling her. "Jenny Villiers!" And then the little miracle happened. For a wonderful moment she hesitated, turned and looked about her in a bewildered fashion, before hurrying into shadowy air.

His heart swelling and pounding, Cheveril stood there in the middle of the room, swaying a little, with eyes closed. When he opened them again, he saw that the lamp on the desk and the lights on the wall near his chair were clear and steady. A door clicked, and a widening wedge of light, whiter and harsher than any he had seen since he had been left alone in there, entered the room. Otley was there.

"Were you calling me, Mr. Cheveril?"

He was confused. "What? No, I don't think so. I mean, I'm sure I wasn't."

Otley sounded dubious. "I thought I heard you calling—that's all."

"I must have been dreaming . . ."

Otley was staring curiously at him. "You're sure you're all right, Mr. Cheveril? You don't want me to get hold of Dr. Cave?"

"No, of course not," Cheveril told him, with a

68

touch of irritation. "I'm all right, thanks. I must have dozed off. And then—wandered out of my chair . . ."

"Well, I won't disturb you, until your London call comes through." And Otley compressed the wedge of harsh white light, and then vanished with it. Left alone again with the dusk and the shadows, bewildered, shaken, and no longer feeling drowsy, Cheveril carefully returned to his own corner, and settled himself once more into the big armchair. This time he did not close his eyes at all. He felt more than merely wakeful. He had that sick nervous feeling, jumpy about the head and crawlingly empty down below, which he remembered from so many First Nights. He was at once excited and apprehensive, and quite incapable of real thought. Something he had not experienced for years, years of wandering in a circle in a dry wilderness, was now plucking at his nerves, a feeling that there was magic about. Somewhere in this desert of his, it seemed, there was a deep cool well under green leaves. It might be the mirage that arrived before the approach of death. It might be life again at last. He picked up the absurd booklet that Otley had shown him, and held it up to the light of the desk lamp behind him. *Jenny Villiers, A Tribute and a Memoir.* . . . The deep silence settled round him. The room waited. . . .

7

A *Tribute and a Memoir—by Augustus Ponsonby Esquire, Honorary Secretary of the Barton Spa Shakespearean Society.* . . . Cheveril was still staring at the title page.

"Yes, sir," said a plummy little voice, "Augustus Ponsonby——"

"What?" cried Cheveril, and pushed himself up from his chair. For a moment there was nothing to be seen, but then there slowly emerged from the dark of the top alcove the figure of a plump bewhiskered little man, who was seated, nursing a tall

70

brown hat. " . . . Honorary Secretary of the
Barton Spa Shakespearean Society, and an in-
veterate and most enthusiastic playgoer, sir."

Cheveril, moving forward a little, found he
could take this absurd apparition quite calmly.
"No doubt you were. But you're not my idea of a
ghost, my friend." But of course Augustus
Ponsonby was not talking to him.

"Well known in the town," Ponsonby continued,
with a rich complacency, "and no doubt known to
you, I trust, Mr. Stokes, as a staunch supporter of
Mr. Ludlow's talented Company here."

Yes, he was talking to the old actor, John
Stokes, who now became visible too. And it might
almost have been old Alfred Leathers in a costume
part. They both had the same battered humorous
look and the same fruity accent.

"Heard of you often, Mr. Ponsonby," Stokes
was saying. "And no doubt you've often seen me."

"Of course, of course, Mr. Stokes. Delighted to
make your acquaintance." And Ponsonby *was*
delighted, you felt. "I cannot imagine what the
company would do without you—such versatility,
such strength, such experience!"

"An old actor, Mr. Ponsonby." Stokes rolled it
out magnificently. "After more than forty-five
years, a man learns how to carry himself through
five acts—and a farce——"

"And carry other people too sometimes, eh, Mr. Stokes? Ha Ha Ha! You've seen some great nights in the Theatre, I imagine, sir."

"I have, sir. And they'll never come again. In my time, Mr. Ponsonby, I've played with Edmund Kean, Charles Kemble, Liston, Mrs. Glover, Fanny Kelly——"

"Great names, Mr. Stokes, great names!" Ponsonby was enchanted.

"Ah—the Theatre *was* the Theatre in those days, Mr. Ponsonby," said Stokes in his richest baritone. "It was all the public had and so we all did our best for it. None of your panoramas and dioramas and Apollonicons and the rest of 'em then. It was the *Theatre* and the Theatre as it ought to be. Now they'll go to anything. Just a rage for silly amusement, Mr. Ponsonby. And it's all money, money, money. I tell you, sir, the Theatre's dying—and though it may last out my time, thank God—I don't give it very much longer. The old spirit's gone. The plays aren't the same, the audiences aren't the same, the actors aren't the same." And he heaved a giant sigh.

"No doubt you're right, Mr. Stokes," said little Ponsonby, looking worried. "As an amateur I wouldn't venture to quarrel with your experience. Yet I called here specially this morning to tell Mr. Ludlow that many of us amateurs and patrons here wish to congratulate him on his Company's new acquisition—Miss Villiers." And now he was nodding and smiling again, like a pink little Mandarin.

Old Stokes put on a look and assumed a tone that he must have often used as a stage con-spirator, and all he needed was a black cloak folded about one arm and raised almost to eye level. "I'm glad to hear you say so, Mr. Pon-sonby," he began. "Miss Villiers has only been with us a few weeks but we're all very pleased with her. Plenty to learn yet, of course, that's only natural. I've given her a few pointers meself. She's apt to be restless and won't keep her head still. But genuine talent there, sir, and a most pleasing personality, and ambition of the right kind too—a young lady with a future, sir. At least, if the Theatre had a future, which I doubt."

Mr. Ponsonby coughed delicately. "Would it be possible for us to see Miss Villiers in some leading Shakespearean roles——?"

"Rehearsing 'em now, sir," Stokes roared, "rehearsing 'em now. In fact—well, here they are."

And they were—Jenny, Julian Napier and Walter Kettle, with their prompt books. The soft gold light that came from nowhere now filled most of the room, and Cheveril found himself much closer to it than before, almost in it. The sense of the gap in time between them and him was still with him, but he was not so strongly aware of it as he had been before. Somehow the whole scene was much nearer, as if the gap were closing.

"Hello, Ponsonby!" cried Napier, with enormous condescension. "You're not supposed to be in here at this time of day."

The little man was embarrassed. "I was looking for Mr. Ludlow——"

"He'll be round at the *Lion*."

Stokes intervened. "I'll take you there, Mr. Ponsonby."

"Jenny," said Napier, smiling, "may I introduce Mr. Augustus Ponsonby—one of our most enthusiastic patrons——"

"And——" he bowed—"also one of your greatest admirers, Miss Villiers."

Jenny was modest. "I'm afraid I haven't done anything here yet worth admiring, Mr. Ponsonby. But perhaps soon—with any luck——"

"It's not luck but hard work," said Kettle harshly. "And we ought to be working now. You'll have to excuse us, Mr. Ponsonby."

"Oh—yes—of course—I'm so sorry——"

"Come along," said Stokes, "we'll go round to the *Lion*. You don't want me for an hour, eh, Walter?" And off they went.

The three who remained were silent for a few

moments. Not one of them was really at ease. It was Jenny, after a quick glance at the other two, who broke the silence. "Rather a sweet little man."

Napier shrugged his broad shoulders—he was a well-built youth, and to-day was very fine in a black stock, a brown coat and pale yellow trousers —and said loftily: "He's a pompous little ass really. But he runs some sort of Shakespearean Society, and they're good for a hundred seats on a benefit night——"

Kettle turned on him. "He may be rather pompous, but he's not an ass—and something better than a buyer of seats for benefit nights."

"Why, Mr. Kettle," said Jenny, smiling at him, "you're very bad-tempered this morning. What's the matter?"

Poor Kettle showed all the self-imposed sick misery of a man in love who had lost hope. "I'm sorry, Miss Villiers . . . too much work prob-ably . . ." he muttered. . . . "I didn't mean . . ."

"Well, you needn't work here, Walter," said Napier carelessly. "You can go down to the stage. I can take Jenny through our scenes. That's why we're here."

Kettle was all hot-eyed mumbling misery. "I don't know about that——"

"What?" And Napier drew himself to his full

75   F

impressive height, towering above the round-shouldered and downcast stage-manager. "Are you insinuating that I'm not competent to take Miss Villiers through scenes I've played hundreds of times? Why you——"

"Julian, please," cried Jenny, giving herself away in her haste to prevent a quarrel. Then she smiled at Kettle. "I know how busy you are, Mr. Kettle—and I did ask Julian specially——"

"No, you didn't," Kettle told her, roughly. "For I overheard *him* asking *you*."

"I was going to ask him."

"But I was first, that's all," said Napier. And he looked at Jenny, and she looked at him, and then they were lost together, a world away from Kettle, who made a sharp turn, not to see them looking like that; and now he seemed very near Cheveril, not only in space but in time and feeling too. And this moment, when Cheveril found himself staring again into Kettle's hollow eyes, suddenly and strangely halted that morning of a hundred years ago, brought the scene to a standstill, so that the three of them were frozen and motionless and silent there, like figures in a stereograph.

"So you were in love with her too." And Cheveril could not have decided, then or later, whether he actually spoke to Kettle or merely directed his thought at him. "And hadn't a chance. Hoped to teach her all you knew about acting—and I have an idea you were the man here who *did* know—and probably did teach her too—but never had a chance, not a hope. I wish I could talk to you properly, Walter Kettle. There's something of *me* in you. I know exactly what you're feeling. And soon it'll be worse for you, much worse—poor devil. Go on, there's nothing you can do."

The whole little scene appeared to give a shiver, and movement and sound and life returned to it. The long-lost morning went clicking on its way, carrying the three of them to their destined ends.

"All right," said Kettle bitterly, hunching his thin black shoulders. "I'll leave you. You have your prompt books."

"Yes," said Napier, grand and careless, "though I doubt if we shall need them."

"I doubt it too." And Kettle moved into the darkness.

The light on Jenny and Napier was a trifle dimmer after Kettle had gone, as if he had taken a little of it away with him. There was a mystery here that Cheveril never fathomed. For this was Jenny's life, of that he was certain, and all the magic moved around her. So why should Kettle sometimes seem so important to him?

The two were rehearsing now the Second Act of

Twelfth Night, and Napier playing the Duke in
rotund style: "Come, hither, boy——"

"I cross there—um?"

"Yes. Not too quick. Now then—'Come hither,
boy——' " and all went well until Jenny, as Viola,
had replied: "A little, by your favour," and then
she broke off.

"Oh, Julian, please—don't look at me like that."

He seized her hands. "How can I help it? And
what does it matter?"

She struggled a little. "Because—oh—we ought
to work. We oughtn't to be thinking about
ourselves."

He was triumphant. "So that's what you were
thinking too."

"No," she protested, "I don't mean——"

"Yes, you do," masterfully. "And *you* can't help
it either." He took her in his arms, and began
whispering. "My darling Jenny—my sweet, sweet
Jenny—I love you. I worship you. I can only
think about *you*."

"Julian, you hardly know me yet——"

"I've known you for ever. And don't call me just
Julian—dearest."

"Dearest," she whispered, "I think—I love you
too."

All the time the light had been shrinking and
fading and the old brown dusk of the unlighted

corners had been creeping nearer, so that both of them—but especially Napier—began to lose substance and definition, until at last, with their whispering hardly more than a faint far sighing of the wind, they were like lovers on a worn tapestry, mere ghosts entwined. Yet Cheveril could see him slowly lift up her face, a delicate glimmering oval, could see her arms creep round him, and could see their lips, dark curves from which all the warm red had vanished, coming together; and heard himself harshly crying: "No, no, no!" Then there was an instant rush of night, with a cold wind roaring in it; and of those two, lovers lost and gone long ago, there was no trace.

Still conscious, in one safe fragment of his mind, of a room that had a corner in it lighted for him, he stumbled back to his chair. The night and the roaring of wind, in which a hundred years were blown away like dead leaves, had not left him yet. But after a fashion he was still capable of thought. Why had he cried "No, no, no!" so vehemently, surprising himself by his urgency? First there had been a deep sense of pity, with some hint of loss mixed with it, and then this girl had come floating out of the past, a past that had never belonged to him, with an odd stir of magic about her. But he had not felt the faintest desire to possess her himself, in no matter what ghostly sense; and

79

there had been no jealousy behind his cry. Was it merely that he wanted to call a halt to the tragic little tale, which insisted upon playing itself again for him? Had he been stripped down, in this hour of naked despair, to man's last and most secret desire, to do what the priests have said God Himself cannot do, to change the past? But what gave this dead girl—girl, wraith, or symbolic figure of a recurring dream, it didn't matter which— her strange significance for him? Even when he had caught sight of her name in a reference book, weeks ago, his nerves had quivered at it, and for a moment he had suddenly gone cold. What mysterious part of his being, of whose existence he had never even guessed, was involved here, among these ghosts of an old theatre? He cared nothing now, as he had frankly confessed to Pauline, even for the Theatre of his own time, which for the last twenty-five years had brought him a living, friends, admirers, some fame. Then why, at this hour, should he find himself emotionally entangled —and that was what was important and not whether he was dreaming or seeing and hearing ghosts, whether he was using his dramatist's imagination or actually visiting the past—in the pitiful little history of an obscure and forgotten actress who died young, this Jenny Villiers? But at the very sound of the name, which he found himself repeating several times, something happened that he realised he had been sadly missing these past years, a stir of magic, an unfolding of the rose in the darkness, the distant flash of a fountain in the desert. . . .

8

AND now, although he could still feel the chair supporting him, he was no longer in the Green Room, not even in the theatre, but outside somewhere, and, he could swear, a hundred years away. An old black wind went roaring in the night. He could distinguish nothing at first, but he could hear the *clop-clopping* of horses pulling their carriages. Then some singing somewhere, as if a sudden gust had torn at the open window of a tavern. Now there were faint lights, lamps dimmed by muslin and blurred by rain. Old

ghosts in old streets. Or was he the ghost now? He
was visited by a sense of panic, as if he himself, not
the weary solid body resting in the chair, but the
experiencing part of him, the spirit, might be
blown away and lost in this old night like a scrap of
paper. He called for Jenny to reveal herself,
demanded to know where she was and what was
happening to her. And it worked.

He was looking, as if through the uncurtained
window, into a drab little sitting-room, in-
adequately lit by one small lamp. Jenny, still
wearing the plain brown dress, was standing by a
horsehair sofa, on which the actress with the snub
nose and auburn ringlets was lolling and yawning,
half-way to bed in her soiled pink wrap and curl-
papers. It was very late, but Jenny was still going
through her Viola speeches, much against the will
of the other actress. Cheveril could hear everything that was said, but it was faint and far away,
much farther removed from him than their
appearance.

"I see you what you are—you are too proud . . ."
Jenny brought it out almost through clenched
teeth. She was tired, far more so than the other
young woman; but she would not allow herself to
recognise the fact. Her eyes were too big and
bright; and shadows had crept into the delicate
hollow of her cheek. She went on, doggedly:

83

"But if you were the Devil, you are fair.
My lord and master loves you: Oh, such love
Could be but recompensed, though you were
                                    crown'd
The nonpareil of beauty!"

The other girl, stifling a yawn, prompted her:
"How does he love me?"

"With adorations, with fertile tears——" But
Jenny broke off. "No, that's not right, is it?" And
clearly she was referring to the way in which she
had said the line.

"Sounds all right to me, dear," said the other,
with a huge indifference.

"No, it isn't. I remember now—

With adorations, with fertile tears,
With groans that thunder love, with sighs of fire."

But although she waited, no cue came. "Go on,"
she cried impatiently. "Sarah, please!"

"Do you know what time it is?" Sarah demanded. "It's nearly two o'clock."

Jenny was half impatient, half apologetic.
"What does that matter? No, I'm sorry, Sarah
darling. I know you're tired. But I must go
through it again. Now then——"

"*Your lord does know*—and so and so and so—
might have took his answer long ago." And Sarah
yawned once more.

84

"If I did love you in my master's flame,
  With such a suffering, such a deadly love,
  In your denial I would find no sense;
  I would not understand it."

And Jenny was coming to life now, not merely saying lines.

"Why what would you?" Sarah cued her.

Jenny continued:

"Make me a willow cabin at your gate,
  And call upon my soul within the house——"

And then she stopped, frowning.

"No, not like that, my dear," Cheveril found himself saying, as if at rehearsal. And then the little miracle happened again, as if for a brief moment she was somehow aware of him.

"No, that isn't right," she said, and then threw herself into the whole speech, speaking it as Cheveril longed for her to speak it:

"Make me a willow cabin at your gate,
  And call upon my soul within the house;
  Write loyal cantons of a contemned love,
  And sing them loud even in the dead of night;
  Holla your name to the reverberate hills,
  And make the babbling gossip of the air
  Cry out, *Olivia*. Oh, you should not rest
  Between the elements of air and earth,
  But you should pity me!"

85

"Pity *me*, you mean," said Sarah crossly. "Keeping me up until this time! I don't know why you should want to bother."

"Because I must, I must. There's so little time."

As she said this the little room was already farther away from him and much dimmer, and the voices in it were dwindling to a tiny whisper.

"I suppose you and Julian have been spooning instead of rehearsing," said Sarah.

"Sarah!" Jenny gasped.

"Oh everybody knows about you two. Talk about babbling gossip of the air——"

"No, Sarah, don't—please don't talk. I'll go back—there's so little time——"

Yes, so little time; and now the lighted window had retreated to a mere distant glimmer and the lines that Jenny was saying again were so many ghosts of words trembling in the dark air:

". . . Oh you should not rest
Between the elements of air and earth,
But you should pity me . . ."

For a moment or two he felt he was floating in the night high above the town, with the wind sighing *Pity me, Pity me;* but then he was leaning his head against a smooth warm wall; and then he was not standing up at all but sprawling, and the smooth warm wall had turned into an armchair.

86

9

THIS time, perhaps because Jenny wasn't there, everything was simpler and plainer, a homely bit of magic, not her kind at all. It started in a different way too. At one moment he was looking across at the opposite alcove, which contained the tall glass case that held, among other things, Jenny's gauntlet glove. And he saw the glass case too. He sat steadily there, no floating, no drumming in his ears by Time's battalions, and looked hard at the glass case, which reflected a little of the light from the wall bracket above his head. But these reflections changed; they came much nearer; they took on a different shape and another quality of light. And then they were reflections in the corner of a snug Early Victorian bar: well-polished brass and pewter, shining taps, the green-and-white china barrels of gin, the bottles catching firelight and sunlight. Then a fat landlord, with a great meaty face and forearms, was there, leaning on his own mahogany. And so, on the other side of the bar, was Mr. Ludlow, in a purple frock-coat and check trousers, and with him was a seedy fellow wearing a hairy tall hat at the back of his head. They were raising glasses of spirits to each other. It appears that the seedy fellow was a local journalist.

"And what you want to say is something like this. Um—let me see." Mr. Ludlow thought for a moment. " 'Following the phenomenal and un-precedented success of Miss Villiers, and—er.' "

The journalist had heard something like this before. "And at the special request of many distinguished patrons," he suggested.

"Certainly. Put that in. Then—er—— 'Mr. Ludlow announces a Grand Benefit Performance for Miss Villiers on Friday the Ninth, when she will play one of her favourite roles, Viola in *Twelfth Night*, with Mr. Ludlow himself as Malvolio and Mr. Julian Napier as the Duke. The evening will

88

conclude with a brand-new screaming farcical item entitled *Catch-'Em-Alive-O.*' "

"A-ha!" cried the landlord, with a wealth of meaning.

"Same again, George."

"A-ha!" But it had a different set of meanings this time. He busied himself with the drinks.

" 'By kind permission of Colonel Baffer, etc,' " Mr. Ludlow dictated, " 'the Band of the Fifteenth Dragoons will be in attendance to render selections during the intermissions. Free List entirely suspended——' "

"Got that," said the journalist, who had been making a few notes. "Nobility and gentry?"

"Certainly. 'Nobility and gentry have already secured a large number of seats, and the public is advised to make immediate application——' You know, the usual——"

"Yes, of course. Prices up?"

"Certainly. 'Owing to the very large demand and in order that Barton Spa should have an opportunity of paying a generous tribute to the work of this gifted young actress——' You know. Pile it on, pile it on." He raised his glass.

"Pleasure to do it," said the journalist. "Your health, Mr. Ludlow."

"Same here. Matter of fact—and no nonsense—she's the best I've had for years. Works hard too, and doesn't even drink." He turned now, for a messenger had arrived, to hand him a large envelope. When Mr. Ludlow had opened it, he gave a whistle.

"Now listen to this, my friend," he began. "Here's a bit of news for you." He read the card he had taken from the envelope. "Mr. Augustus Ponsonby presents his compliments to Mr. Ludlow, and on behalf of the Barton Spa Shakespearean Socity, invites Miss Villiers, Mr. and Mrs. Ludlow, Mr. Julian Napier, etc., to a late reception and supper at the *White Hart* Hotel, after the Grand Benefit Performance for Miss Villiers on Friday the Ninth." Mr. Ludlow swelled with enthusiasm and pride. "There you are. Read it for yourself. Didn't know it was coming. Great compliment."

"A-ha!" said the landlord, with a different meaning again. Leaning there on his bar, he seemed to be able to express himself adequately without using words at all.

Mr. Ludlow swallowed the rest of his drink. "Well, there it is. All ready for a nice half-column in your *Bartonshire Chronicle*. And now," he added, with immense gusto, "to work—to work." And he swung round, made a move straight towards Cheveril, and promptly melted into thin air. The bar glinted and glimmered a moment longer, and then was gone too.

IO

CHEVERIL felt far less tired now. Energy and zest were welling up from some unknown source whether chemical or psychological, or both. He took a few turns about the room, from light into shadow, shadow into light. A certain excitement, of a kind he had not known for years, possessed him. He felt the sense of a great occasion. And then after a few minutes of this restlessness and vague excitement, it occurred to him that he was being infected by the mood of the theatre itself and all the people in it. But which theatre, which

91   G

people? Merely to ask was to know. He had
slipped back again. He was feeling what they had
all felt one night in 1846. Yes, it was the Grand
Benefit Performance. And most of all he was
reflecting Jenny's feeling. But where was she?

He saw her, as it were, at the end of a short
tunnel, running obliquely down to her dressing-
room. She was wearing a wrap and staring into a
lighted mirror at her make-up. He had time to
notice, among the flowers on her table, the green-
and-scarlet glove. And from far away, as if
through a closed door or two, were coming all the
backstage noises, cries along the corridors, and the
sound of distant music. He knew she was shaking
with excitement.

Julian Napier, already in his costume as the
Duke, had come in, carrying some red roses. Their
voices, quite clear but tiny, came up the tunnel to
him.

"Julian, thank you, my darling. I was hoping
you would, but thought you might be too busy to
remember. Darling!"

"You're never out of my thoughts a moment,
Jenny. I love you."

"I love you too." She spoke gravely. He kissed
her but gently she pushed him away. "No, please,
darling. Not now. They will be calling us in a
minute. Wish me luck for my great night!"

"I am doing, all the time. And I feel it'll be my success too. I shan't be jealous."

She was simple enough to be surprised at this. "Of course not. I knew that. Darling, there isn't much time."

"Listen then." He spoke in a quick whisper. "You're staying in the hotel too to-night, aren't you? What's the number of your room?"

"Forty-two. But——"

"No, my darling, please listen. You must let me come to you after all these fools have finished talking. It's our only chance to be alone together. And I want you so terribly, my love. I can't sleep. I can't think properly. Sometimes I feel I'm going mad——"

"Oh Julian, I'm sorry——"

"No, I'm not blaming you, of course. But to-night, it can be *our* night, at last. Room Forty-two. I'm along the same landing. Nobody will know."

She was hesitating. "It's not that, darling. It's —I don't know what to say——"

"Of course not. I don't want to press you now. But give me a sign, when we're with those idiots at the hotel. Look, if you give me one of these roses I've brought you, I'll know it's all right. Please, my darling."

She laughed. "You *are* a baby. All right then."

They were calling: "Overture and beginners, please. Overture and beginners."

"We're being called," she told him. "I must hurry."

"Don't forget," he warned her. "One red rose— and you'll make me happy."

Cheveril saw her nod and smile and then turn to her mirror again, but already the images were blurred and fast dissolving, as if he were staring down through water over which a shadow was creeping. For a few moments longer he thought he could hear a far distant sound of music and then applause. Then there was nothing at all. He was simply standing in the silent darkened Green Room, imprisoned within the Now. Perhaps there was nothing more to be seen and heard. The ghosts had done with him. Or the time-track refused to curve itself for him but remained a fixed stiff length, which meant that a century away might just as well be ten thousand years.

Resentfully, he returned to his chair and took up the booklet, which was all he had now. There he read slowly: "Never will those of us who were privileged to be present both at the Theatre Royal and later at the *White Hart* Hotel that evening, forget the occasion. An audience which included nearly all the nobility and gentry of the neighbour-hood filled the theatre from pit to ceiling, and

94

every entrance and exit of the brilliant young actress was lustily applauded. A more delightful Viola was never seen—though of that, more later. Then afterwards there was the reception by the Shakespearean Society at the *White Hart* Hotel, where the writer had the honour to make the first speech, in praise of the chief guest of the evening, upon whose radiant charm no shadow of forthcoming early doom was yet cast. Miss Villiers," said the writer . . .

But the light on the page had gone, and the soft golden glow, fuller than he had known it before, had stolen into the room. But into which room? This was not the Green Room into which he was staring, although its dark panelled walls were much the same. There was a long table, rich and gay with flowers and fruit, decanters and bottles glasses dark with port or winkingly bright with champagne. On the near side were several empty places and through this gap in the centre he could see Jenny, radiant behind her red roses, and the Ludlows and Julian Napier. On each side of them, reaching so far that they were lost in shadow, were nobility and gentry and Shakespeareans in the tremendous evening dress of the Eighteen-Forties. Standing there, and beaming above an immense starched and ruffled shirt-front, all pink and glorious, was little Augustus

Ponsonby, clearly making the most of his moment.

"Miss Villiers, on behalf of the Barton Spa Shakespearean Society, I wish to offer you—and Mr. and Mrs. Ludlow and all the members of Mr. Ludlow's Theatre Royal Company—our most grateful thanks for the pleasure, the delight, the intellectual and spiritual satisfaction you have given us during this season, which, illuminated by the lustre of your dazzling performances, has undoubtedly been the most memorable season that Barton Spa has had for many, many years."

There were cries of "Hear, hear!" and some applause, during which Jenny looked demure; though Cheveril knew at once that she was clearly aware of the little man's absurdity, which shone through his pompous oratory.

"Time after time," Augustus Ponsonby continued, warming to his task, "to eyes softened by your genius, you have appeared before us in the veritable guise of those bewitching products of the teeming fancy of our Immortal Bard. You have offered us the very lineaments and the authentic enchanting tones of an Ophelia, a Rosalind, a Viola. It is hard for us to believe that genius married to such youth and beauty will be content much longer to hide itself from the—er—gaze of metropolitan audiences——"

"Now, now," Mr. Ludlow called to him,

"don't put ideas into her head, Mr. Ponsonby."

"Of course not, Mr. Ludlow," said Ponsonby hastily. Then he returned to his grand manner. "I merely wished to observe—er—that we of the Shakespearean Society are aware of our good fortune and that is why we have taken this opportunity of offering Miss Villiers our homage and most grateful thanks. And now I call upon Sir Romford Tiverton to propose the Toast."

There was much applause, during which Cheveril saw Jenny flash a sparkling look at Julian Napier. Then Sir Romford Tiverton rose, holding up his glass. He was a fantastic, be-whiskered old buck, who might have wandered out of one of Thackeray's minor burlesques.

"Mr. Charman—an' fwends," said Sir Romford, "it is with vewy gweat pleashah—that I wish to pwopose the toast of our beautiful and talented guest of honah—Miss Villiers—coupled with the names of our old fwends—Mistah and Missis Ludlow——"

"Miss Villiers!" All but Jenny and the Ludlows were standing and cheering now. But the sound they made seemed to Cheveril to be much farther away and much fainter than their appearance, and came to him as a kind of midget enthusiasm that gave a touch of sad irony to the whole scene. "Speech—speech—Miss Villiers!" they were crying.

97

Jenny was dismayed. "Oh—must I?"

Ponsonby was almost severe. "Of course you must."

"Go on, me dear," said Ludlow. "Just something short an' sweet."

"Well, ladies and gentlemen," said Jenny. "I can't make speeches, unless of course somebody writes them for me and I learn them off by heart. But I'm very grateful to all of you for helping to make my benefit such a wonderful success, and for entertaining us here. I've never been happier in the Theatre than I have here at Barton Spa. Appearing on the stage, as I'm sure you all know, isn't all fun and glitter and applause. It's hard and sometimes heart-breaking work. And we're never as good as we'd hoped to be. The Theatre is like life all—well—packed up in a little gold box, and like life it's often frightening, often terrible, but *wonderful*. The only thing I can say—except *Thank You*—is that I'm only one of a company, a very good company too, and that I owe a great deal, more than I can say, both to Mr. and Mrs. Ludlow——" But she remained standing while they clapped. "And also to our brilliant leading man, Mr. Julian Napier." And as they clapped again, she tossed one of her red roses to Napier, who caught it and kissed it.

It was then that the third miracle, the most

staggering one, happened to Cheveril. She still stood there, vivid and alive, but all the others might have been figures in a dim old photograph. Not a sound, not a movement, came from them. The moment out of long ago had been suddenly arrested, its time jerked to a standstill; but Jenny herself was free of this moment, this time, as if she could act and communicate in some other and mysterious dimension. She looked vaguely in Cheveril's direction, and spoke straight out at him, though in a low intimate tone.

"You see, I *had* to throw him the rose. Poor Julian!—he kept looking so downcast, so wistful. They were all making such a fuss of me and hardly noticing him. And I wanted him to be happy too. You understand, don't you?"

"Are you talking to me?" said Cheveril.

"I'm talking to somebody who's here now, who wants to understand me, but who wasn't there when it all first happened."

"When it *first* happened?"

"It all goes on happening. You can get back to it, if you think hard about it, although it's never just the same——"

But a shiver passed over the scene, and movement and sound returned to it, and Jenny was finishing her speech of thanks. "So—ladies and gentlemen of the Shakespearean Society—on behalf of us all at the Theatre Royal—I thank you again. *Good my lords, you have seen the players well bestowed.*"

She sketched a curtsey, and sat down, to prolonged applause, which was finally silenced by Augustus Ponsonby, who commanded Mr. Ludlow to address them.

Mr. Ludlow rose ponderously, the noblest Roman of them all, his face an imperial purple. He was probably drunk, but he had a manner and style that came to terms easily with liquor. "Me friends," he began, rolling a little, "from the bottom o' me heart, I thank you. You have—to continue the quotation from *Hamlet*—used us well, not only here, in this rich an' festive hour, but also in the playhouse itself. For I see around me tonight many familiar faces, and I know that although you are me patrons an' I your humble servant, you will allow me to address you as my friends." The Shakespeareans applauded, and Mrs. Ludlow, like a volcano erupting, burst into tears.

"I have been among you now for many years," Mr. Ludlow continued, "both as an actor and as a manager, and now as I look back from this momentous year of eighteen-forty-six——"

But now Cheveril was conscious of a strange sound, a most incongruous sound, absurd and yet imperative and demanding.

"—A stormy year of much strife at home and troubles abroad," Ludlow observed with relish, "when it might be thought that the Thee-ayter would cease to command the attention of a public concerned and worried about the Corn Laws, the Chartists, the Irish Famine, the wars in Mexico and India——"

It was the telephone, ringing and ringing. For another moment, Ludlow was still there, mouthing and gesticulating, although no more than a thin ghost; and then the next moment he was gone, and Jenny and all the banquet, players and Barton Spa Shakespeareans and all, gone with him; and there was nothing but the Green Room, with the telephone on the desk ringing its head off. Cheveril stared at it in bewilderment.

II

OTLEY looked in, and the light that came through the open door was oddly white and harsh. "Your London call, Mr. Cheveril."

"Yes," he answered, with some confusion. "I thought—I mean, I heard the bell."

"Right then." And the harsh light vanished with him.

Cheveril picked up the receiver rather gingerly, as if the instrument had only just been invented. "Yes, this is Mr. Cheveril speaking personally." And of course they asked him to hang on, the usual result of speaking personally. Perhaps the telephone disliked this personal stuff. As he waited, he found there were still thin tatters and wisps of that scene in the *White Hart* Hotel clinging to his mind. And Jenny, of course. But this was no time to think of her.

Otley, a nice helpful chap but inclined to overdo it, looked in again. "Coming through, Mr. Cheveril?"

"Now they've found me," he grumbled, "they've lost the other people."

"My girl can wait for it——"

"No, thanks. I'll better hang on myself now." He put his other hand across his eyes, like an exhausted and bewildered man. When he removed the hand, he saw that Otley, who had come farther in, was regarding him curiously.

"I don't want to bother you, Mr. Cheveril—but are you sure you're all right?"

My dear Otley, he felt tempted to reply, I have just had a most exciting and intimate little chat with a young woman who died a hundred years ago. But all he said was: "No, I'm not sure."

"Nothing I can do, is there?"

Yes, my dear helpful little Otley, you can explain to me the mysteries of Time, Immortality, the Soul, Dreams and Hallucinations and Visions, the Creative Mind, the Personal and Collective

Unconscious. But he merely replied: "Don't think there's anything anybody can do, thank you, Mr. Otley."

"Easily nip out and get Dr. Cave again, you know. He told me where he'd be—only round the corner."

"No, thanks, don't bother. It's not a case for Dr. Cave—not yet, anyhow." The telephone began asking questions again. "Yes," he told it, "this is Mr. Cheveril, and I think Sir George Gavin wants to speak to me." Otley departed. Waiting now for George Gavin, Cheveril experienced a change of mood. He was almost his usual self again. His feet were back on the ground. He refused to think—this was not the moment for that—but he felt ready to talk to George, even although he was not sure now what his decision would be about those theatres. George Gavin was a rich City man, a solid oldish bachelor, tough in business but forever enchanted by the Theatre, about which he was curiously humble and also unexpectedly knowledgeable, unlike most well-to-do Englishmen who are at once patronising and ignorant about the Theatre. It afforded George Gavin some necessary release and expansion, and although theatrical management was not his profession, he always entered into it with fine zest and was a good colleague, as Cheveril had found more than once. They were, in fact, excellent friends.

"Hello, George! Hell of a lot of fuss, isn't there, when you have to talk on a telephone?"

George said he was telephoning from a restaurant, and added that Cheveril sounded peculiar, not quite himself.

"I dare say I do. I had to take some stuff."

"Now look, old man," and George sounded concerned; but then he always assumed that Cheveril was made of much finer and more delicate clay than himself. "I heard you weren't quite the thing. I can leave this a day or two, you know."

"No, no, go on, George."

"I'll have those theatres by the end of the month," George announced. "All set, old man."

Cheveril said he was very glad, and meant it.

"Thank you, old man," said George, who also meant it. "I thought I'd better tell you, although I know you're busy down there. But there are the theatres—and my offer stands."

"As I said before, George, it's a very generous offer and I'm tremendously grateful for it." He hesitated.

"But?" George prompted him.

"No, it's not *But*. The fact is," Cheveril continued, "I don't know what to say. Earlier

105

to-night I'd made up my mind to refuse your very generous offer, George, simply because I felt I'd finished with the Theatre. Told Pauline Fraser so, and she lost her temper with me."

George said that he sounded less certain now.

"Quite right, George. But I can't say that I've changed my mind. I can't get hold of my mind to change it."

"Say that again, old man," said George earnestly. And when it was repeated to him, he asked if Cheveril had been drinking.

"Haven't had a drink all day. But the doctor gave me some stuff, which I took too much of, and I've been resting and dozing here in this Green Room. And——" and what? His mind raced desperately, to find an answer that was not a thundering lie and yet would do for George Gavin over the telephone. "And—well—I must have been dreaming, I suppose. I don't think I was really asleep, though."

George suggested day-dreaming. "Often happens to me, old man," he added, "especially just after lunch."

"This wasn't just after lunch," Cheveril told him. "And it wasn't day-dreaming either. Too vivid for that. But a kind of dreaming, of course—must have been." And as soon as he had said that, there descended upon him, like a vast grey weight, all the weary sense of futility he had felt while he had been talking to Pauline. But now there was somewhere in it, like an undefined ache, a bitter feeling of loss and regret. And he didn't want to talk to George any longer, and it didn't matter whether they ran the theatres or not.

"You sound as if they've been doping you a bit, old man," said George with sympathy. "Now don't you bother about this business. You've enough on with your play. How's it looking?"

"Pauline and the others are grumbling about the Third Act." He hesitated a moment. "I say, George, is somebody crying at your end of the line?"

"Somebody *what?*"

"Crying."

"Nobody's cried here for years," said George. "More likely to be at your end."

"I believe it is," said Cheveril gravely.

"Now look here, old man, you take care of yourself or we might all be crying soon. And just talk to me about this offer when you feel like it."

"Thanks, George. It may be later to-night."

"I'll be back in the flat fairly early to-night. Or you can get me at the office to-morrow. And take it easy, and mind the ghosts in that old dump don't come after you."

H

"Now what," asked Cheveril earnestly, "makes you say that, George?"

"Just something Pauline said. 'Bye, old man."

As Cheveril brought the receiver away from his ear, he held it for a moment, almost as if weighing it in his palm, and regarded it with astonishment.

12

THERE was of course no sound of crying now. How could there be? He told himself not to be a damned fool. The only thing left to do was to get down into that big chair again, and really to have a rest before attempting the rehearsal. He closed his eyes. He was alone in a dark continent of misery. He couldn't fall asleep and he couldn't bother to open his eyes and be properly wakeful. He was ready to resent being disturbed and yet he found it hateful sitting there alone. Almost better be dead and done with it.

And then he heard her crying, this time quite clearly.

He knew at once, before he opened his eyes, that she was there in the room. But she was hard to see at first, just a thin wraith in the shadow. That hundred-year-old light wasn't there; no deep amber glow coming from nowhere. The place was dark, and although the sound of her choked little sobs was clear enough, she herself was nothing but a faintly phosphorescent transparency, a vague troubling of the shadows.

"Jenny," he called softly. "Jenny Villiers! Can you hear me?"

He could swear now that she was looking toward him, and as he stared until his eyes ached it seemed to him that there was bewilderment in her face. He didn't speak again, for he felt she might vanish altogether if he did.

Then the light was there again, and this was the Green Room of a hundred years ago. She was wearing the plain brown dress he had seen before, and she looked as unhappy as she had sounded. This was not the radiant Jenny of the supper party at the *White Hart*. While he had been talking to George Gavin, a finger had flicked a page or two, and now the last chapter had begun. Not much time left now; it was written among the new hollows in her face; and his heart went out to her.

Kettle, who suddenly appeared, glared hungrily at Jenny and then turned to withdraw, looking more haggard and unkempt than ever. His shabby black had a graveyard mould on it. Death itself might have crept in to take a look at her.

She saw him. "Walter!" He had to turn then. "What's the matter?"

"Nothing's the matter, is it?" he said harshly.

She was ready to cry again. "I see."

"Why do you think something's the matter?" he demanded, pitiless in his love and despair.

"Because we used to be such good friends," she told him. "You were so kind and helpful to me when I first came here, and now you're so bitter and angry, as if I'd offended you." She gave him time to reply, but he said nothing, so she continued: "Have I offended you, Walter? If I have —I'm sorry. I never meant to." She was genuinely humble.

"Take no notice of me," he said. And his contempt for himself was in every syllable. "I shan't be here much longer. And I don't know which has been worse—to see you so happy, as you were at first, with that conceited fool Napier—to see you as you are now—made miserable by him——"

"No, please, don't say that, Walter. It isn't true. If I'm unhappy, he's not making me unhappy——"

"Something is," he said gloomily, not looking at her. "And I can't imagine what else it could be."

"Tell me—I've been wanting to ask this, and you're the only one I can ask. I don't seem unhappy when I'm playing, do I? It doesn't show then, does it?"

He looked at her now. "No, thank God! Haven't you seen me—haven't you *felt* me—watching you from my corner? There you are still, with all your lights blazing, your banners flying. But then, as soon as the curtain's down, you're pining and drooping——"

She was able to smile. "Now that's not true, Walter. I don't pine and I don't droop. You've made that up. Walter—dear Walter—be friends. I need friends."

He took the hand she held out and kissed it, so fiercely that she shrank a little. He stared at her a moment, out of the dark hollows that were his eyes, and then without another word he turned abruptly and vanished among the shadows. She made a movement, as if to stop him, opened her mouth to speak, and then checked herself, fighting hard to keep her self-control. Cheveril was acutely conscious of her despair, which swept over him like a black tide. He knew too, though how or why he could not imagine (unless of course she

112

was his own creation and these very scenes were his), that bad news, all that she secretly feared, was hurrying to meet her.

Yet for the next few minutes the scene was lightened, for the old actor, John Stokes, and Sam Moon, the comic, marched in arm-in-arm, both wearing enormous beaver hats. They gave her a quick glance of affectionate concern, and then each dexterously raised the other's hat. "Your servant, madam!" they cried together.

Jenny smiled. "Be covered, gentlemen!" She was a young duchess in some antique play.

Sam Moon touched her cheek with his forefinger, and then put the tip of that forefinger to his tongue. "Too salty."

"Tears, eh?" said Stokes, looking reproachfully at her.

Jenny shook her head. "Let's talk of something else—at once."

Moon nodded and winked. "Yes, John," he said, in what must have been his stage voice, full of squeaks and grunts, "I used to get a devilish good dinner of stewed beef behind Drury Lane for threepence ha'penny. And for sixpence a man could dine like a lord."

"That's another thing that's wrong now," said Stokes. "Everything costs too much, including actors."

"What about actresses?" said Jenny saucily.

"There ain't any."

Jenny was genuinely indignant. "What? John Stokes, you have the audacity to stand there——"

"Now, now, my dear," said Stokes, half in earnest, "I don't say you haven't the making of an actress, and quite a good one, but it'll take you another fifteen years at least to become what *we* call an actress——"

Her dismay was not all pretence. "Fifteen years! Why——"

Moon stopped her. "No, it's not long. You'd be surprised—wouldn't she, John?"

"You turn round one morning," said Stokes, with a touch of real melancholy, "and then—where are they?"

"Gone!" But this was from Mrs. Ludlow, who had arrived in full sail, quivering with anger or excitement or some strong emotion. "Gone!" she repeated, with tremendous dramatic effect. Behind her were Sarah and the other young actress.

Jenny stared at them, alarmed. "What?"

"Who's gone?" cried Stokes.

"Didn't I say that that low feller, Varley," Mrs. Ludlow demanded, "who came to see us last week, was probably scouting and touting for Mrs. Brougham, who has the Olympic now? Didn't I, girls? And if he's not opening at the Olympic a week from to-day, as soon as they can get the bills printed and put up, then my name's not Fanny Ludlow. Mr. Ludlow and I walked out of the Olympic when Madame Vestris had it. 'Never again,' I said to Mr. Ludlow——"

"But who's gone?" asked Stokes.

"Without saying a word—not even Good-bye. He must have been sitting up with that Varley both nights, demanding parts, settling terms and billing——"

"But who—*who*——?"

"Why, Julian Napier of course. Who else?" She stared at Jenny. "Child, you're as white as a ghost."

"Am I?" said Jenny. She tried to smile, and then fell in a dead faint. Immediately the light and the colour began to fade out of the scene; the brown dusk stole into it; and all the figures there might have been in some old sepia print.

"You men——" and Mrs. Ludlow's commanding tones were already much fainter—"go and get a drop of brandy and some water—and ask Agnes for my *sal volatile*."

He could only just distinguish the three women bending over Jenny. Their voices came to him in fluttering little whispers.

"Better loosen everything. There—there——!"

"Mrs. Ludlow—I think——" And the girl sounded shocked.

"You needn't, Sarah. I know now. And I know now why Julian Napier left in such a hurry."

"Do you think she told him?"

"No, she wouldn't. He guessed—and then ran away. A London engagement—and out of his troubles here. And with both of them out of the cast, I don't know what I'm going to say to Mr. Ludlow. . . ."

The three women bending over the still figure might have been wisps of smoke. But as these dissolved, and the last faint mutter of speech went with them, Cheveril felt that the Green Room itself vanished too. Once again he was somewhere outside, in or above the town, but it was as if a dim old film were being raced through the projector, so that it was impossible to understand what was happening. Time was compressed, and so all sights and sounds, while ghostly thin, were blurred and confused. But he had an impression of rain, cold dark rain in narrow streets; and with it a feeling of anxiety that was almost anguish. Oh lost, gone and lost, lost for ever, as time flickered by in the cold horror of the rain!

13

IT was steadying itself. There was a glow, like a distant fire in the night. There were sounds that gradually became words. Firelight and lamplight were playing on bottles and tankards. It was the cosy corner of that tavern again, late at night now, with the same landlord leaning on his bar and the same seedy journalist talking to Ludlow. They were raising their glasses.

"Your health, Mr. Ludlow!"

"Same here. Though if it wasn't practically doctor's orders now," said Ludlow gloomily, "I

117

doubt if I'd touch it. Haven't the heart for it, you might say. You tell me that some patrons are complaining——"

"Afraid they are, Mr. Ludlow," said the journalist apologetically. "We've had one or two letters, in fact, but I thought I'd mention it before printing 'em."

"Very friendly of you. The same again, George. I ask you," cried Ludlow, with sudden fierce despair, "I ask you—what can a man do? Without a sign or a warning or a by-your-leave, it all comes at once. Napier—breaking his contract, mind you —sneaks off to London——"

"Where I hear he's having a big success at the Olympic," said the journalist.

"Possibly, possibly—never a very discriminating audience." Ludlow condemned them in one impatient wave of his hand. Then, back to despair. "When he goes, Miss Villiers, around whom I had built my season, instantly collapses. Her distress at being abandoned in this fashion, for she was a wife to the fellow in all but name, aggravates her condition—and—well—you may have heard——"

"Yes, I did," replied the journalist, with an air at once mysterious and knowing. "I thought at the time it was better that way, probably——"

"So did I. But when that's over, instead of picking up, she gets worse, steadily worse.

Doctor's tried everything, but no use—no use."

"Sort of decline, eh?"

"Yes. Week after week, a slow ebbing away," said Ludlow, not without genuine concern and yet enjoying himself. "And everybody in the Company aware of it, talking about it, haunted by it. What's a man to do, sir? I ask you—what *is* a man to do?"

"Nothing. Have another. Same, George."

And now Kettle was there, soaking wet, looking haggard and desperate. Cheveril could feel Kettle's misery like an ache in his own body. It was queer, and never to be understood by him then or afterwards, how the scene lost its mere theatrical quality and became terribly alive for him, plucking at his nerves and crushing his heart, as soon as this man came into it. His sympathy with Jenny he could understand if not fully comprehend in all its mysterious aspects. She was the lovely doomed girl, around whom his imagination had first played; it was she who had conjured him into these glimpses of lost years; she could be anything; a dream figure lit with his own neglected tenderness and shadowed with his own regret; the smiling magical mask of an archetype; the Theatre itself, as he consciously refused to see it, entering the dark little stage door at the back of his mind in this exquisite pitiful guise. But why this man, this Walter Kettle, this thin black grotesque?

"They wouldn't let me see her," Kettle was saying bitterly. "She's obviously worse. But that old fool of a doctor won't say anything. I waited, to speak to him. But it was useless. He doesn't know what he's doing or where he is." He took his glass of spirits from the landlord, and swallowed the raw stuff in one shivering gulp.

"Or where poor Miss Villiers is either, eh?" said the journalist, and would have said more but Ludlow touched him on the arm.

Kettle looked through him rather than at him. "I know where she is. She's at death's door. Queer phrase that, when you come to think of it. Death's door," he repeated slowly.

"Walter, my boy," cried Ludlow, "this won't do. You're wet through—and shivering. You'll be going down next."

"Not I," said Kettle contemptuously. "I'll burn my time out. This town's like a steaming graveyard to-night. I felt we were all dead and just didn't remember. That old doctor's nothing but a fat old corpse falsely resurrected. Another, George."

"A-ha!" said the landlord, quite faintly this time.

"And when you've had that one," said Ludlow, "you'd better run along to your lodgings and get to bed, Walter. You're a sick man yourself."

Kettle laughed. It made a harsh grating sound, with too little blood and too many dry bones in it. "Of course I am. We're all sick men. You—with your painted faces and painted scenes. This fellow here—with all the solemn lies he prints. And even George there, who poisons us so that we don't notice too much on our way to the graveyard. That's where we're all going, gentlemen. And a pleasant journey to you!"

Cheveril felt himself going out into the rain and darkness with Kettle, and the firelit corner of the tavern might have been blown out like a candle flame. There were no streets and houses but just night and cold rain and misery. The sun and all our happiness had set for ever. And Hell wasn't somewhere else, cheerfully crackling and roaring away: it was here, in the sodden black night, and every moment, with hope gone, was a thousand years of it. And then there was a vague impression of a yellow oil lamp hanging high at a corner; of Kettle, who had had no food all day and whose stomach was queasy with raw spirits, leaning against the dimly-lit wall, sick with misery; of some tall-hatted "Peeler" stopping to stare and growl; of Kettle reeling away into the dark, sloshing along the gutters, slipping on the greasy pavements, hungry for life, love, art and glory and yet longing for death. And this was not Martin Cheveril, who had coolly accepted so much, who believed in so little, who had never been the drudge of some minor old playhouse, half-starved and desperately overworked, who had never burned himself away in some daft ultra-romantic passion, who had never thought and felt like a man of the Eighteen-Forties: this was that poor foolish wraith, Walter Kettle. Yet in those mysterious moments Martin Cheveril thought and felt as he did, suffered with him as he had never suffered with any creature of his own invention, and even began to recognise some profound changes in himself. . . .

14

NOTHING now. No Theatre Royal nor tavern, no Walter Kettle, no rods of rain in the streets of old Barton Spa. The uneasy darkness might still be a hundred-year-old night or merely the border of sleep. Was this the end? And if not, where was Jenny Villiers? He called her name several times, with increasing urgency, and was not surprised that he was calling it aloud, as if to the Green Room itself, to the tall glass case, the watercolour sketch, the booklet, the gauntlet glove.

Jenny Villiers

Her voice when it came was small and quiet, coming from nowhere in particular, a little voice out of the shadowy air. She said: "It was very lonely—dying."

"Lonely?" He made it sound like an echo.

"Yes, very lonely," she said slowly and simply, as if a disembodied voice must be very patient with its listeners. "Everybody seemed a long way off. It was the loneliest thing that had ever happened to me."

"Were you frightened?" he asked her very gently.

"No, I wasn't frightened. I think I was too tired to feel frightened. But I was lonely—and terribly sad—until the very end."

"Until the very end?" Did he actually say it or merely think it? "After weeks and weeks in some dreary little back room, far away from the lights and music and applause, feeling lonely and sad . . . wasted hands and hollow cheeks . . . great burning eyes and bright hair . . . what happened then, my dear?" There was no reply. Nothing. But this could not be the end; he couldn't allow it to be. He was on his feet now, crying urgently: "Jenny, if it was better, not so terribly sad, at the very end, I must know. Make me see. Let me listen. Jenny, what happened? Do you hear me?"

It was a small bedroom, lit by two guttering candles, which threw huge shadows. Jenny, with her hair loose, was sitting up against a mound of pillows; she was wasted and very pale. A stout old nurse, hardly more than a thick shadow herself, sat at the bedside. There was a dull sad drumming of rain on the roof.

Jenny was pointing to the candles. "You know what we used to call them?"

"Yes, dearie. Candles. They're only candles."

"No, not just candles. Not when the wax has all run down the sides—thick white wax running and melting away. We used to call them winding sheets. That's true, isn't it? Winding sheets."

"Now you've not to talk like that, dearie. Only just 'ave patience, and we'll 'ave you better in no time. You want to act in the thee-ayter again, don't you?"

"Yes, of course." Jenny's wandering mind was alarmed. "What time is it? I mustn't be late. I must get dressed. Why am I lying here?"

The nurse leaned forward to restrain her. "Now—now—you can't go to-night, dearie. You're too poorly—and any'ow it's too late."

"Yes, it's too late," Jenny muttered. "Far too late. . . . *Goodnight, ladies; goodnight, sweet ladies; Goodnight . . . goodnight . . .*" Her voice died away, but after a moment or two she heard something that startled her, and made a sudden movement. "Listen—what's that noise?"

"Only the rain, dearie," said the nurse. "The West wind's bringing the rain to-night."

"*Heigh-ho—the wind and the rain.* . . . That's sad too. I don't know why it should be, but it is. And he meant it to be, you know. *But that's all one, our play is done.* . . . It's pretending not to be sad, not to care at all, but all the time it *is* sad. It makes me cry."

"Don't you let it then, dearie. You needn't bother your 'ead about it."

But Jenny was alarmed again now. "Yes—yes— I must. And there isn't much time. . . . What does it matter how late it is, Sarah? I know you're tired, but I must go through it again. *Make me a willow cabin at your gate.* . . . *And call upon my soul within the house* . . ."

As she sank back, exhausted, a tall figure, its height exaggerated by a long black cloak, made its appearance by the bedside, as if Death had arrived at last. This doctor, who might have been designed to fill the space he occupied in the most effective sombre fashion, completed the picture, which might have been a melancholy low-toned Academy triumph of the period. This dying girl of the theatrically romantic composition, with her fading tangle of hair, her hollow cheeks, her eyes burning

with delirium, was not Jenny herself, but Miss
Villiers in her last great role. And Walter Kettle
himself might have set the scene and sketched in
the appropriate dialogue.

"I'm afraid she's weakening fast, doctor," the
nurse whispered. "And her poor mind's a-
wandering again."

Jenny opened her eyes wide and slowly smiled at
the doctor.

"Now, Miss Villiers," he said quietly.

She shook her head, like a child. "I'm afraid
I've been a great trouble to you, doctor."

"No, you haven't, Miss Villiers."

"Yes, a great trouble. . . . Where's Nurse?
. . . Has she gone?"

"No, I'm still 'ere—bless you!"

"I can't see you," she said faintly. "It's dark.
. . . Why is it so dark? . . . And what's that
noise?"

"Only the rain, dearie."

"No—no—listen!" And Jenny, with a last
effort, was sitting up.

And Cheveril found that he could hear it all too
—the music far away and then the sound of distant
applause, and then a young voice, coming nearer
and nearer, calling *Overture and Beginners, Overture
and Beginners!*

"My call," said Jenny, smiling and triumphant,

127

"my call." And as she sank back, a black wind came roaring out of the huge darkness, and the whole scene curled and withered, as if it were a leaf and all autumn had been compressed into a moment; and like a leaf it was blown away. Then once again there was nothing.

15

So there it was—*Curtain—The End*. He had set
this queer evening in motion, whatever the
mechanism might be, by remembering a brief
entry in a reference book: *Jenny Villiers, Actress,
died Fifteenth of November* 1846, *aged* 24. And that
was all; there could be no more. He could hear
again Otley's casual tones: "Jenny Villiers came
here from the Norfolk Circuit, and got some
leading parts. She fell in love with the leading
juvenile, Julian Napier, but he suddenly left the
company for a London engagement. Then she

was taken ill—and died. And Napier didn't last much longer. He went to New York, started drinking hard, and soon finished himself. That's all there is to it, really." There was the voice of reasonable history and sound commonsense. Jenny Villiers yesterday, Martin Cheveril to-day; and every year the first dark wind of winter stripping the trees of their last withered gold—no wonder that little death-bed scene was blown away like a leaf.

Yet in the middle of her speech at the supper in the *White Hart* she had stopped and had then apparently spoken curious words to him. Well, that must have been his own most elaborate imaginative effort. But because there obviously could be no Jenny Villiers talking outside time as we knew it, because that must have been himself talking to himself, some mystery still remained. What self was this that masqueraded, so vividly too, as a long-dead actress, and addressed his conscious mind in this strange fashion? And what hidden reservoir of energy and zest and renewed delight, which were themselves a kind of magic, had been tapped at this moment? He had seen a fountain sparkling in his desert then, and where was it now?

Rapid chemical effects in the blood, he decided, remembering Dr. Cave's tablets, of which he had taken four instead of two. And those tablets and chemical effects, which had the power—no mean power either—of staging fantasies in some corner of his brain, had apparently done all they could do for him. His dry weariness was returning fast, and round him stretched the desert and its old white bones. He opened his eyes and took a careful look at the Green Room, and there was no mistaking it for anything but the Green Room of the Theatre Royal, Barton Spa, that was closed this week but would open on Monday (*Special Engagement! Free List Entirely Suspended!*) with the world-premiere of Martin Cheveril's *The Glass Door*, with Full West End Cast. The room was now quietly staying in its proper place on the time track. It was ordinary Here and Now. This, he admitted, was reasonable, and as it should be; but as he closed his eyes again, he found himself giving a sigh so deep that it was almost a groan.

It was echoed by a sigh that was still deeper, even more like a groan, with something theatrical, affected, about it. A figure in black, walking along a dim corridor, had turned to receive, from another and even vaguer figure, a number of letters and notes. Then a door opened, into a brightly-lit space, and the figure in black, framed in the open doorway, became Hamlet Prince of Denmark. And Hamlet was grumbling, with no suggestion of real displeasure, because so many

131

ladies compelled him to read their gushing
tributes, after the performance, and hinted at
possible assignations.

The dressing-room was very different from
Jenny's modest little cubbyhole in the Theatre
Royal, Barton Spa. This was for the leading man
at the Olympic Theatre, London. There was a
fine large mirror, brilliantly lit, above a table gay
and luxurious with flowers, cut glass and decanters.
The carpet, the sofa and chairs were dark crimson.
And Julian Napier, in his Hamlet costume, over
which he now threw a loose silk dressing-gown,
looked very handsome and distinguished, very
much the London leading man. He was humming
cheerfully and smiling, and was clearly delighted
with himself and the world. He tossed the letters
and notes on to the table, poured himself out a
generous helping of brandy, and sat down in front
of the mirror, to begin removing his make-up.
There was a knock.

The man who entered was plump, middle aged,
and had a sallow face, longish hair and a blue-
black goatee beard. He had a solemn and emphatic manner, a long cool stare and a slow nasal
drawl, and was obviously an old-style Yankee.

"Mr. Julian Napier," he began, portentously.

"Yes, sir." Napier was haughty. "And who are
you?"

"Jacob G. Mangles, sir, of New York City," he replied, producing a card. "Favourably known to Mrs. Brougham and all the leading managers of your city, Mr. Napier."

"You were in front to-night, Mr. Mangles?"

"I had that pleasure, Mr. Napier, and allow me to congratulate you upon your presentation of the Noble Dane. A ree-markable smart performance, Mr. Napier."

"Thank you, Mr. Mangles. Will you join me in a drink?"

"Not at present, sir, thank you, as my friend Mrs. Brougham is expecting me in her office. But I want to tell you, Mr. Napier, that two hundred thousand of our best citizens—and a right smart heap of dollars—are eagerly awaiting, at a word from Jacob G. Mangles, to see you as Hamlet—and as anything else you desire to play— on Broadway and elsewhere. Name your terms, Mr. Napier."

Napier smiled. "Well, that's very good of you, Mr. Mangles. But I don't think I want to visit America just yet."

Mr. Mangles consulted his watch. "I cannot keep a lady waiting, Mr. Napier, but later, if you are still in the theatre——"

"I have a supper engagement, Mr. Mangles, and I too do not like to keep a lady waiting——"

"In less than quarter of an hour, Mr. Napier, I will put to you a proposition for a season in my New York theatre that will eternally astonish you by its liberality."

"I'm not like to change my mind in the next ten minutes—still——"

"Stranger things have happened, Mr. Napier. I guess I'll take a chance." And off he went.

Napier was amused. After taking another pull at his brandy, he applied himself in earnest to the task of removing his make-up. He was wiping the last traces of grease from his darkly handsome face when his next visitor arrived, bursting in without any warning. It was Walter Kettle, looking wilder and more haggard than ever, almost a scarecrow figure.

"Walter Kettle!" Napier was astonished. "What's brought *you* to London? Left old Ludlow at last?"

"She's dead, Napier," cried Kettle, fighting for his breath. "And you killed her."

Napier rose, and towered above him. "I don't know what you're talking about. Who's dead?"

"Jenny's dead."

"Jenny Villiers?"

"Yes—yes—yes—dead—dead!" Kettle was like a madman now, and was clutching at Napier and glaring and shouting. "We're burying her the day after to-morrow. And—by God!—you killed her, Napier, you and no one else, just as surely as if you put a bullet in her heart. You killed her——"

"Let go, you dam' fool," Napier roared, "or I'll break your arm." He threw Kettle off, sending him reeling across the room. Humiliated and exhausted, Kettle leant against the wall. "What happened? I didn't even know she'd been ill. *Has* she been ill?"

"Yes," Kettle muttered. "It started the morning she discovered you'd left us." He breathed hard, painfully.

"Well?" Napier demanded impatiently.

"She was going to have a child, you know."

"Of course I didn't know. She never told me."

Kettle did not look at him. "Well, she didn't have it. And then she never got better. I don't think she tried. Your leaving us like that finished her. You killed her, Napier. And I'll never allow you to forget it as long as I live." But there was no force, no real menace in the threat.

"Forget it? D'you think I'm going to need you to remind me?"

"Whether you'll need it or not, I'll remind you." And now Kettle did look at him.

It was this look that brought Napier across the room in two fierce strides. "Don't try to take that tone with me, Kettle. I'm in the mood to ram it back down your throat. I acted with her—I loved her—I lived with her. Just remember that."

"And you left her."

It was curious how this dialogue, although delivered with a fierce sincerity, reflected the kind of Theatre both these men knew so well. They were themselves, most passionately too, and yet the effect was as if they were still playing parts, as if this dressing-room was itself on the stage of some mysterious greater theatre.

"I left her," said Napier, speaking carefully now, as if he had to justify his actions to himself as well as to Kettle, "because I wanted this engagement here. It was too good a chance to miss, and I knew that if I told her she'd persuade me not to accept it—to wait until we were offered a double engagement. You all knew where I was, and when she didn't write, I thought she was angry—as she'd a right to be, no doubt—and had done with me——"

"She was too proud to write——"

"Yes, yes, I can understand that," Napier told him impatiently. "You haven't to explain her to me." And then he hesitated a moment. "How did she die?"

"Sadly." Kettle was very grim. "An inch a day."

"Drop that," cried Napier, in a sudden fury, "or I'll——"

"I thought you wanted to know."

"Well," said Napier, "now I don't want to know." Then he was angry again. "Get out." And as Kettle did not move, he shouted again: "Get out—and leave me alone." He swung round, and then flopped down on the chair facing the mirror.

Kettle went slowly to the door, where he turned. "Good luck for the great career, Napier," he said softly. "It's going to need plenty." And was gone.

Napier finished his drink in one gulp and hastily poured himself out another and larger one and soon swallowed that. He had started on a third drink, and was now already half drunk, when Mr. Mangles returned.

"Now, Mr. Napier, just in case you might be interested in a right smart proposition——"

Napier jumped up, glaring at him. "Yes, yes. You want me to act for you—and all your thousands of best citizens——"

"I certainly do, Mr. Napier."

"Hamlet—Macbeth—Othello——"

"All the great roles, Mr. Napier."

Napier's voice dropped to a strange whisper. "All right, Mr. Mangles. I'll act them out of their damned seats. By God, I'll give 'em such a picture of fear and terror and remorse that it'll haunt their dreams. A drink, Mr. Mangles, a drink—eh?"

137

"Well," said Mr. Mangles, smiling, "I could use a little liquor."

"You could use a little liquor, eh?" he cried as he filled the glasses. "Well, use that. And drink to my appearance on your Broadway——"

"With pleasure, sir. You have the style our citizens admire, Mr. Napier."

He was obviously drunk now. "I have—have I? Well, we shall see."

"Now, sir, as to terms——"

"Damn the terms! Talk to me to-morrow. I'm in no mood for terms to-night." And he pointed a shaking forefinger at his visitor, and declaimed with drunken passion:

> "I loved Ophelia; forty thousand brothers
> Could not, with all their quantity of love,
> Make up my sum——"

And he sent his glass crashing against the opposite wall.

Mr. Mangles was the appreciative showman. "Very fine, Mr. Napier. Now our people, sir, are romantic and spiritual-minded——"

"Then, by Heaven, Mr. Mangles!" cried Napier wildly, "I'll have to charge you more, and you'll have to put the prices up—if we're all going to be romantic and spiritual-minded together. No—no—Mr. Mangles," he added, as the other tried

138

to interrupt, "to-morrow—to-morrow—talk to me
to-morrow——"

He flung himself down, with his head on his
hands on the dressing-table, and sobbed in a dry
choking fashion. Mr. Mangles gave him a shrewd
look, put down his glass, and quietly walked out.
Napier remained motionless and unseeing before
the mirror.

The dressing-room began to fade for Cheveril,
who thought: So that's how it was. Well now, I'm
sorry. And did she know—could she know—what
happened to you, my friend?

It was only the thinnest ghost of a scene now, but
he could still see Napier with his head buried in his
hands, among the grease-paints and small props
and letters and flowers and glasses and decanters,
with the mirror gleaming faintly above him. And
then it seemed as if there was something forming
in the depths of the mirror—a white image—a face
bent in pity—Jenny Villiers. . . .

16

IT was the Green Room again, of that he was certain. But was it the Green Room now or the Green Room then? Were the two glass cases and all the portraits there? And what about the other door, the one that had vanished sometime since 1846? The brown dusk was deeper in tone and thicker than it had ever been before, almost like a dark fog. And Cheveril did not know what to do. If he concentrated too sharply, using the razor edge of consciousness, everything might suddenly clear, once and for all, and he would find himself fixed in the present moment, with nothing left but a portrait and a glove, a name and a few pitiful little historical facts. But if he allowed his attention to drift into this brown sea-fog of time, he might never encounter her again. This was the most important moment of all, for which everything that had gone before was merely a preparation. Jenny! The cry came from his heart, which neither knew nor cared whether this was a girl who had escaped from her death and the bounds of her years or an image from his own deeper self. Where was she? Jenny Villiers!

Not a sound. Not a flicker of light in the dusk. Nothing but a dark and blurred suggestion that the Green Room was still there. And no mere weariness held him now, but a huge bleak misery that might soon sharpen to pain. If he had lost her now, if this dull confusion was the end, then it would have been better for him if he had died an hour ago in this chair.

"Jenny!" he cried alone, with a great urgency, as if it had been long arranged, warmly discussed between them a hundred times, that they should meet in this place and at this very moment; and that here he was, at last.

The reply came, there in the Green Room with him: a peal of laughter, ringing clear as a silver bell.

141

The old light, with its mysterious amber glow, spread through most of the room, and only a small ring of shadow separated him from it. He saw the last and strangest of all the scenes revealed to him that night. First, Jenny herself. She was looking young and gay in a white gown, much as she did when Kettle had first brought her in; and she was standing in what appeared at first to be a doorway, with more light playing about it than could be seen elsewhere. It was, too, a different kind of light. It was as if she stood at this end of a narrow and short corridor, which led out into brilliant sunshine, with some of it finding its way down the corridor and dancing and sparkling around her head. She stood there in some enchanted Maytime of her own, as if newly arrived from the great golden world that has for ever haunted men's imagination. Yet this was no doorway that framed her, Cheveril saw, but the tall mirror fastened to the wall in the top alcove, a mirror, much used in the old days by the players, that had survived all the changes of the Green Room. It was the familiar mirror, yet now it was a doorway too, for there she stood, gracefully poised on the very edge of it, and mysteriously transmitting so much of the light coming from behind her that all else in the room appeared subdued and dim.

They were like figures in an old daguerreotype, the Ludlows, Stokes, Sam Moon and the rest of the company. They all wore dark clothes, and sat huddled, motionless, listening gloomily. It took Cheveril some time to understand what was happening, for just as they seemed nothing more than dim worn monuments of death when compared with Jenny's dazzling and pulsating life, so too any words spoken among them were the dullest faint muttering after her peal of laughter. There was, however, an anxious little middle-aged man seated facing the assembled company, and gradually it dawned on Cheveril that this was a scene that must have taken place very often in the old green rooms. It was an author reading his new piece to the company. And his name, it appeared, was Spragg, and he was reading one of the dreadful little farces of the period, which were used to conclude the programmes, and it was called *Mr. Tooley's Tarradiddles*. And the only one there who was enjoying it—for the wretched Spragg was now in despair—was Jenny, who was laughing and occasionally clapping her hands together, unseen and unheard by all the others.

With the desperate over-emphasis of a despairing author, Spragg was hurrying towards his final curtain:

143

"*Mr. Tooley:* 'No, ma'am, I have to confess that I never had a brother and if I had had a brother I wouldn't have behaved like that to him.'

"*Mrs. Tooley:* 'Aunt Jemima, it was just another of Mr. Tooley's tarradiddles."

"*Comic business with parasol again——*"

And Spragg looked round at them like a drowning man, but added, hoping against hope: "Very effective."

"Yes," cried Jenny, "I can see her. Go on, Mr. Spragg. What's the curtain?"

Spragg quickly searched the faces of the company for some faint sign of appreciation, found not a glimmer among them, and so hastily continued:

"*Aunt Jemima:* 'Well, me dear, I can only say Thank goodness it's you who's married to the man and not me. But I'll not cut you out of me will this time, 'cos I'm truly sorry for you, married to such a fool!'

"*Mr. Tooley:* 'I deserve no better of you, ma'am, but in future I'll remember to *tarry* before trying to *diddle* again.'

"*Aunt Jemima:* 'Gracious—what's that?' "

Again it was Jenny, whose interest in this monstrous composition appeared to be quite genuine, who cried: "Farmer Giles, again?"

"*Entrance of Farmer Giles down chimney, covered with soot*," Spragg announced, and added, with a last despairing glance at the players: "Very funny effect this, bang on the curtain." There was no response, and after a deep sigh, he continued:

"*Mrs. Tooley:* 'Why, it's poor Farmer Giles!'

"*Farmer Giles:* 'Yes, and black in the face after listening to Mr. Tooley's Tarradiddles.'

"*Gives great sneeze—all strike attitudes—Tableau—Curtain—End of Farce—Mr. Tooley's Tarradiddles.*"

And Spragg flung down his manuscript, mopped his brow, and tried to look as if he were a thousand miles from the glum troupe in front of him.

"I loved it, Mr. Spragg," cried Jenny. But only Cheveril heard her.

"Thank you, Mr. Spragg," said Ludlow gloomily. "Very funny, I'm sure."

The wretched author gave him a heart-broken look. "Mr. Ludlow," he began, with a hint of tears in his despairing voice, "I don't know if I've been reading badly—but I do assure you, on my word of honour, this farce took famously both at York and Norwich, where they're all hard to please. Of course you have to *see* it."

"Yes," said Sam Moon mournfully, "some good comic business there—specially Farmer Giles——"

This exasperated poor Spragg. "But—dash my

buttons!—you never laughed once—not one of you——"

"Oh what a shame!" cried Jenny. "Poor little man! Letting him read all that—and nobody laughed at anything but me." And now Cheveril began to wonder if she was talking to him too. Certainly he alone heard her and knew she was there.

"Tell him, Mr. Ludlow," said Mrs. Ludlow mournfully.

"Tell me what?" Spragg shouted, still exasperated.

Mr. Ludlow looked very grave, and his tone was solemn. "I have a confession to make, Mr. Spragg. I asked you to come and give us this reading of your new piece a week or two ago, as you know. I forgot to cancel your visit, and then hadn't the heart to tell you when you arrived here——"

"Tell me what? You're not closing, are you?"

Mr. Ludlow was shocked. "No, no, my dear fellow."

"We were closed last night, Mr. Spragg," said Mrs. Ludlow in her deepest contralto, "because we had all attended the funeral of our leading female juvenile, whom we all admired and loved dearly— our poor sweet Jenny Villiers——"

Spragg was at once dismayed and reproachful.

146

"Oh—I say! Now really, ma'am——"

"And this is the first time the company's met since we all said good-bye to her for ever——"

"No, no, darling," said Jenny urgently, "it isn't like that at all."

"We're feeling it, Mr. Spragg," Mrs. Ludlow sobbed, "we're feeling it most deeply——" And the young actresses sobbed too, while the men blew their noses hard and looked sternly at their boots.

"No, look," said Jenny, "it doesn't matter a bit. Please!"

The whole scene, figures and faces and voices, was beginning to fade rapidly now. Already it was like the dimmest old film that had gone round and round in the projector too many times.

"You ought to have told me, y'know," said Spragg. "Not fair, upon my word!"

"I know we ought," Mrs. Ludlow told him tearfully. "But we thought you might be able to make us forget."

"But there's *nothing* to forget," cried Jenny.

"It's no use, Jenny," Cheveril found himself telling her. "You're a ghost even to ghosts now."

She looked at him and replied to him: "No, I'm not."

The others were so many whispering and mumbling shadows in the gathering dusk, above which Jenny's face was still clear and bright.

Said the little actress, Sarah: "We can't forget her . . ."

Said old John Stokes: "It'll take some time yet, I'm afraid . . ."

Said droll Sam Moon: "The heart's right out of us, you might say . . ."

Jenny protested: "No, Sam, John, Sarah, all of you. It doesn't matter about me. Nothing's been lost. And all that matters is—to keep the flame burning clear."

"The best in this kind are but shadows," murmured Cheveril.

"They're going," cried Jenny, in some distress. "They're going again." And indeed the players were nothing now but a thickening of the dusk and a low mumbling there.

He found that he was standing only a little way from her, although he could not remember moving from his chair. He was staring at her face above the mumbling dusk. No light fell on it from the room, but it was still vivid, like a transparent mask seen against a brilliant illumination. Perhaps it was more like a mask now than a living face. Yet her voice was still troubled, warm and sweet, a woman's voice and not some false hollow echo of his own thoughts.

"You tell them it doesn't matter about me," she

said, "or about anybody, so long as the flame burns clear. *You* know."

"How should I know?"

"You did once. Tell them."

"Too late, they're gone," he said. "And it was all long ago." And no sooner had he said this than he saw, with dread in his heart, that the dusk was beginning to creep up and to obscure Jenny herself now.

"No, not long ago." Her voice was much fainter, and the warmth and eagerness were leaving it. "Still now, if you want it to be."

"You can see me this time?"

"Yes," came the whisper, "I can see you."

"Because we're both ghosts."

"No, it's not like that. Why are you pretending not to understand?"

"Why should I understand?" he asked gently. "And why did you say I knew once?"

He could still see her face, overshadowed though it was, but he could only just catch her reply, it was so faint. "Because—we talked. Don't you remember?"

He moved forward a step or two, but it brought her no nearer.

"And don't try to find me—yet."

He called in anguish to this hollow fading ghost: "Jenny! Jenny Villiers!"

Her voice was a world away. "No . . . not yet . . . not yet . . ."

There was a last glimmer of a face, no more than if a glow-worm were near an ivory mask; and then darkness. But he cried to it: "Jenny, let me see you once more, just once more, and then I shall know. Just once, Jenny!"

She was standing there, as she had been at first, in the bright gold of her enchanted Maytime, and it seemed to him that her lips moved to pronounce his name. He sprang forward with arms outstretched and made her name a great exultant cry; but even as he moved the shining image faded; and it was the dead cold mirror into which he crashed.

"The Glass Door!" he shouted, even as the very floor swung at his head like a hammer. "Only the Glass Door!"

17

. . . THERE were lights; too many lights; and all with a nasty trick of rapidly contracting and expanding. There used to be plenty of quiet steady lights, so why this nonsense now? He tried to put a tongue to the question, couldn't manage it, and then found something exquisitely comical in the whole idea and had a great desire to giggle. Two immense figures, with faces like wobbly pink balloons, were with him; and in fact they were bending over him.

One of them said: "It's all right, Mr. Cheveril.

151

The doctor's here." And then turned neatly into Otley, a decent little chap. But there were more important things to think about than Otley. Oh yes—of course!

"The Glass Door," he told them. "The Glass Door."

"What did he say?" This was the doctor. Yes, Dr. Cave.

"*The Glass Door*," said Otley. "That's the name of his play."

"Oh yes. Mind running on it, you see," said Dr. Cave. "That's what happens with this type. That's why one's got to take risks with 'em."

But they had missed the point about the Glass Door. But what was the point? He tried to remember, but couldn't.

"Now then, Mr. Cheveril, feeling better?" This was the doctor, using his loud cheerful professional tone.

"Yes, thanks," said Cheveril, slowly and carefully. "Sorry about this." He tried to sit up. "But I was all right, you know . . . and then when I moved towards her—she vanished . . ."

He was able to notice the look that Otley gave Dr. Cave, and then he saw the doctor shake his head. They were both an ordinary sensible size now, and though he still felt that the Green Room was too brightly lit, for every light was on, there was no longer anything queer about the place.

"Was it that mirror up there?" he asked.

"That's where we found you," said Otley. "I'd heard you shouting something about a glass door."

"Well, a mirror's a kind of glass door, isn't it?" said Cheveril. But he knew now it was no use talking to them.

"You did a neat little dive into a complete black-out, Mr. Cheveril," Dr. Cave told him. "Well now, suppose we get you back into that comfortable chair, eh? Do you feel you're ready to make a move now?"

He was, with some assistance from them, and then he was back in the deep armchair. He smiled at them. "I won't try to explain. You wouldn't believe me if I did. But I'm sorry to have been such a nuisance."

"Don't worry about that," Dr. Cave told him. "Fortunately, Mr. Otley took a peep at you about half-an-hour ago, and thought you were looking queer, and so very sensibly telephoned me."

"I'm much obliged," he said to Otley.

"Not at all, Mr. Cheveril. But I'd better get back to my office. You can give me a buzz from the desk here if there's anything I can do for you."

After Otley had gone out, Dr. Cave lit a

cigarette, plumped himself down on the little chair that was too small for him, and gave Cheveril a long and rather quizzical look.

"I've given you an injection of coramine. You had a shocking pulse. I took rather a chance before, but with people of your type, one has to make allowance for the way your minds are working. No good telling you to rest if you're not ready to rest, you just fret yourselves into a worse state. Well, the coramine will keep you going for a few hours, if you've anything you want to attend to urgently, but after that you'll either rest properly or find yourself another doctor."

As the doctor was talking, Cheveril discovered two things about himself. He was feeling fine, better than he had done for a long time; and there was in fact a startlingly new effect of energy and zest in him. Then there were various important things that he wanted to do and that ought to be attended to as soon as possible. So he said: "Thanks, Doctor. I'll do whatever you want me to do. But there are certain things I'd like to get on with, first. And I shan't be able to rest until I do."

"So I thought." Dr. Cave made a long arm and took the bottle of tablets from the desk, and looked at it thoughtfully. Then he looked at Cheveril. "You took two of these?"

Cheveril frowned. "Yes. I followed your instructions!"

"Sure you took only two?"

"Why, yes. I distinctly remember taking two and swallowing them with some water. Wait a minute, though." He stopped to think. "No, I took four. Not deliberately. I took a second two, forgetting that I'd already taken two. I say—I'm sorry."

"Don't apologise to me," said Dr. Cave, a grin on his large red face. "Apologise to yourself. That was asking for trouble. What probably happened was that you gave yourself such a boost that your heart couldn't take it." He gave Cheveril another grin. "What does it feel like to be nearly dead?"

And then Cheveril remembered. "Not yet," he said slowly.

"What's that?"

"It's quite different from what you might imagine. Perhaps we go from one kind of time to another. You come to an end in one, but then move off, like moving into another dimension, in another sort of time."

"You've been dreaming."

"I wonder."

The doctor took a final pull at his cigarette and then stubbed it out in the ashtray. "If you'd just put a little more strain on your system, my dear

L

sir, you'd have dropped clean out of any kind of time for good and all."

Cheveril smiled at him. "How do *you* know, Doctor?"

"Well, I don't," he replied, getting up. "My job is to mend bodies—and yours needs looking after." He held up the bottle of tablets. "I'll take these, by the way. So, without unduly exerting yourself, just attend to anything here that you feel you can't leave, and then ask Otley or one of your company to see you back to your hotel, go to bed and stay there until I see you again. That'll be some time in the morning. And don't worry if you don't sleep too well to-night. And don't take a sedative—just lie quiet. Good-night."

"Good-night, Doctor," Cheveril called after him. "And thank you. By the way, you might tell Otley to look in for a moment, if you see him." And the doctor, almost out of the door, gave an acknowledging wiggle of his black bag.

Cheveril looked slowly and searchingly round the Green Room, at the two glass cases, the furniture, the portraits, the tall mirror in the alcove. It was the same room that he had dismissed with a weary glance earlier in the evening. Yet it was not the same room, for then it had been dead, and now it was alive. Or he who looked at it had been dead and now had come to life again.

Now he stared about him in wonder and tenderness and strange joy. An eagerness he had not known for years possessed him. So little time, as time was reckoned here, and so much to do, first in this very room, and then in the wide glittering world outside, so terrible, so wonderful. It did not matter much what a man attempted, with so many fine things to be done, but still he was fortunate, for he had his profession, his workshop, his glorious golden toy, the Theatre. . . .

18

"Y ES, Mr. Cheveril?" said Otley.

"Two things, if you don't mind." And then he hesitated a moment.

Otley was smiling. "You're a lot better already, aren't you?"

"I believe I am. Well, now. First, ask your secretary to get through to Sir George Gavin—the number's Regent Six One Five O. He may not be back there yet, but leave a message for him to ring me here as soon as he can—it's rather urgent."

Otley was making notes. "Yes—got that. Anything else, Mr. Cheveril?"

"Well—you remember that young actress who wanted to see me——"

"Ah, I'm sorry about that, Mr. Cheveril. She just slipped past us."

"No, that's all right." He cleared his throat. "I refused to see her. Well, I was wrong. And if she comes back, I insist upon seeing her."

"All right, Mr. Cheveril," Otley replied dubiously. "But it isn't likely she will come back."

Cheveril stared at him without seeing him. "You know, I think she might," he said slowly. "The last thing she said—and I thought it odd at the time—was 'You'll be sorry soon you said that.' That was after I told her to clear out. And she was quite right. Now I *am* sorry."

Otley still looked dubious. "Still—that wouldn't bring her back, would it?"

"I don't know. It might. She also told me to be careful."

"Careful about what?"

"Ghosts, I think."

Otley laughed. "Oh—well—it's like I told you, Mr. Cheveril. You know how superstitious they all are."

"Are you?"

"No, no, not me."

159

"I believe," said Cheveril slowly, "I am."

And then old Alfred Leathers came waddling in, through the door that led down to the stage. "Not interrupting anything, am I?"

"No, come in, Alfred."

"I'm not wanted on the stage for a spell," said Alfred, panting a little, "so I just came up to see how you're getting on."

"We were talking about ghosts. And I was about to remind Mr. Otley that we're ghosts too."

Otley smiled. "Now, now, Mr. Cheveril, none of that. Well, I'll get your London call put through as soon as I can, and I'll tell 'em down at the stage door to let that young woman come up, if she does come back."

By the time Otley had gone, Alfred Leathers had drawn up a chair near Cheveril's and was sitting there quietly ruminating. Cheveril regarded his battered old trouper's face with affection. They had often worked together, and there was more than one Second Act curtain and tricky Third Act in a Cheveril play that old Alfred had negotiated with his solid technique and long experience. And now as he sat there, an old actor glad of a short rest, he reminded Cheveril of somebody else he had met recently.

"Alfred, do *you* believe we're ghosts too?"

"I know I often feel like one."

"That's not what I meant, you old scoundrel."

"Then I wouldn't know what you mean." And Alfred sighed gustily, and stared hard at a bunion that threatened to burst out of his left shoe. "But what *I* mean, Martin my boy, is that I've been acting too long—and—as the youngsters like to say —I've had it."

"Nonsense, Alfred!"

"No, no. Mean what I say. In fact, the Theatre's had it. We've had one or two hold-ups on the stage this last hour, and Pauline and Jimmy Whitefoot and I have been arguing a bit, in that nervy way we have during last rehearsals. And I think you're right—and they're wrong. The Theatre's finished and we might as well admit it." And he wagged his massive old head.

Cheveril did some wagging too. "It was different," he said smoothly, "when you were young, of course—eh?"

"Different?" cried Alfred, at once expanding. "I should think it was."

"You've seen some great nights in the Theatre, I imagine, Alfred, eh?" It was like a prompt.

"I have, Martin. Great nights. And they'll never come again. Don't forget that in my time I've played with Irving, Ellen Terry, Tree, Mrs. Pat."

"Great names, Alfred!"

"Ah—but the Theatre *was* the Theatre in those days, Martin. It was all the public had, and so we all did our best with it. None of your films and radio and television and the rest of 'em *then*. It was the *Theatre*—and the Theatre as it ought to be. Now they'll go to anything——"

"Just a rage for silly amusement——"

"You've taken the words out of my mouth," cried Alfred. "Yes, silly amusement, old boy. And it's all money, money, money——"

Cheveril wanted to laugh, but he continued prompting: "The Theatre's dying—though it may last out your time——"

"Yes, thank God! But I don't give it much longer."

"The old spirit's gone," said Cheveril with mock solemnity.

"Right! The plays aren't the same——"

"The audiences aren't the same——"

"And the actors," said Alfred; and Cheveril finished it with him, "aren't the same."

"Here, I say," Alfred added, "this is a duet."

Cheveril smiled at him. "Well, you see, Alfred, I know that speech about the dying Theatre. I've heard it before, to-night."

"Not from me you haven't, old boy."

"No, but from somebody rather like you," said Cheveril slowly, "only he was talking a hundred

162

years ago, and it was panoramas then and not films, and he'd acted with Kean and Mrs. Glover in his youth instead of Irving and Ellen Terry."

"I don't get you, Martin. Who had?"

"This old actor I heard——"

"Heard? Where?"

"Here in this Green Room. Just the place to hear it."

Alfred looked relieved. "Ah—I see—you've been dreaming, old boy."

"All right, I've been dreaming. But it was the same speech, Alfred. And I realised of course how untrue it was then, and you can see that, because your famous Theatre of the 'Nineties was still two generations away. And I realise it's not true now."

"Half a minute, Martin. That doesn't follow."

"Logically it doesn't, perhaps," Cheveril admitted. "The rumour of a death may be false fifty times and then at the fifty-first may be true."

Alfred gave his right knee a sharp slap. "Exactly. And everything goes to prove——"

"That you're an elderly actor, Alfred, and that the Theatre's dying for you. It's always been dying for the old hands. And it's always being born again for the new ones. And that's not its weakness—that's its strength. It lives—really lives and not merely exists, but lives as humanity lives—just

163

because it's for ever dying and being born, because it's always renewing its life."

"Now what's been happening to you?" And Alfred gave him a shrewd old man's look.

"Dreaming. But we were wrong about the Theatre, Alfred, and the others were right."

He was not convinced. "Now wait. It's dying for me, we'll say, but who is it being born for?"

"Miss Seward's here," said Otley at the door.

"Send her in," Cheveril told him. Then he looked at Alfred. "Your answer's here."

19

SHE was neither tall nor fair, but a square-shouldered girl of medium height, with a wide face and fine greeny-dark eyes. She was no more like Jenny than corduroy green slacks, which were what she was wearing, are like a full flowered-muslin dress. And at a first glance this young Seward girl was not very different from dozens of young actresses he had met during the last few years. What could he have been imagining? There was not the least glimpse of Jenny here. Except, of course, hopeful and buoyant youth itself, and its hint of radiance. But he smiled at her, and she came nearer, as he rose from his chair rather laboriously; and then they were face to face, and she looked straight at him, and he felt a cold pricking along his spine.

"Ah, Miss Seward," he exclaimed rather pompously, trying to gather his wits. "This is Mr. Alfred Leathers."

"How d'you do, Miss Seward?" Alfred presented her with his wonderful old grin. "Actress—eh?"

"Yes, Mr. Leathers." She was rather breathless. "I saw you play that marvellous old waiter in *The Forbidden House*. Will you tell me something?" And she went nearer, as he nodded and smiled encouragement. "That scene at the end of the First Act, when you turned your back to the audience, and stayed quite still—was it your idea or the producer's?"

Alfred chuckled. "It was my idea."

"Well, it was wonderful," the girl cried. "And I'll never forget it."

"Thank you, Miss Seward." He took her small and rather grubby hand into his own great paw. "Nice of you to mention it. And good luck." He turned now to Cheveril. "I think you might be right after all." Then he addressed them both, smiling broadly: "I must go and rehearse."

After he had gone, the other two were silent for a

few moments. Cheveril felt that the room was watching them. He indicated the chair near his, and when she had taken it, he sat down himself. They regarded each other steadily for one queer second. The room waited.

"You were quite right, you know," he began, in a low and rather uncertain tone.

"What about?" she asked, but without any suggestion of surprise.

"When you said I'd soon be sorry I didn't see you before. Now I apologise——"

"No, please don't," she cried warmly. "You were feeling tired and rather ill, weren't you?"

"I was." And now it seemed quite a long time ago.

"And anyhow—here I am." She smiled at him confidently, almost as if they were old friends.

"But what made you say I'd be sorry? How did you know?"

"Oh—it just came into my head—the way things do sometimes, you know."

"You told me to be careful—remember?"

Yes, she remembered.

He looked at her gravely. "Why?"

"You were staying in here by yourself, and I could feel it getting all ghostly. Was it?"

"Yes, it was—afterwards." And then there was a long pause.

"You don't want me to tell you about it." And she made this a statement, not a question.

"I don't want to tell anybody about it," he told her.

She looked at him searchingly. "You're different."

He nodded; and then she glanced round the room, looked at him again, and nodded too. It was as if there were a lot to be said that never would be said now, because there was no need for it. The room would not speak now, and so they, who were both deeply and mysteriously involved with the room, need not speak either. That is how it seemed to Cheveril.

"My other name's Ann, by the way," she announced casually, breaking the spell.

"And so you stayed on in Barton here——?"

"Yes," said Ann. "I felt sure I would see you— and I said to Robert——"

"Who's Robert? The boy friend?"

"Yes. He came with me—and he's waiting below. Poor Robert! He's always having to wait."

"He's in love with you?"

"Yes," she replied, with great solemnity. "And I am with him too. It's been going on for *ages*."

"You mean—perhaps—a couple of years——?"

"Nearly. But don't let's talk about that."

168

He smiled at her. "All right. What about acting? Ever played Viola?"

She nodded. "Just lately too."

"Can you remember the scene with Olivia—the Willow Cabin speech?"

"I'll try." And she got up and stood expectantly.

"Go on." He prompted her: *"Why, what would you?"*

As soon as she began, he remembered a drab little sitting-room lit by one small lamp, shining very late in a dim old night of wind and rain:

> *"Make me a willow cabin at your gate,*
> *And call upon my soul within the house——"*

Then she stopped and looked at him apologetically, and he could feel the cold pricking again, for she had made the same mistake that Jenny made and had stopped where Jenny had stopped.

"No, that wasn't right," she said. "I'm sorry."

He regarded her gravely. "Don't be sorry. I'm not. Now then—*Why, what would you?*"

By the time she had come to the end of the speech, and was crying *"But you should pity me!"*, he was standing quite close to her, staring and wondering. When she had done, she stood there for a moment, silent, staring at him too. They might have been listening to far-away music.

"I don't suppose I did that speech very well," she

169

said, breaking the tension. "I don't think auditions are much good really, do you?"

"Not much," he replied, joining her on the same level. "But they tell you something. You're in Repertory somewhere round here, aren't you?"

"Yes. Wanley. It's weekly rep. I'm playing the leads now. But I feel I've done enough of it."

"You want the West End now, do you?"

"No, not particularly," she replied. "What I do want is a chance to be produced properly and to rehearse properly, after all this tearing weekly rep. Look, Mr. Cheveril, I'm a real actress. I don't want simply to walk on and exhibit myself. I know the stage isn't—isn't all fun and glitter and applause——" She hesitated.

Cheveril tried to conceal his excitement. "Go on, go on. What is it then?"

"Why, it's hard—and sometimes heart-breaking work. And I know we're never as good as we'd hoped to be. The Theatre is like life all done up in a little box——"

"Yes. And like life——?"

"It's often frightening, often terrible—*but wonderful.*" She broke off, and gave an apologetic little laugh. "Oh—I don't know why I'm saying all this to you. It suddenly all came out."

"Yes, I know it did."

"Anyhow, I expect you've heard it all before."

"Once."

She opened her mouth to speak, the question already written in her eyes, but he hastily checked her.

"Let's sit down," he said, and found the cigarettes and offered them to her. After lighting hers, he tried one himself, his first since he had taken the tablets, and discovered that it tasted good. So they sat there smoking, at ease.

"Tell me, Ann, were your parents on the stage?"

"No. In our family it's every other generation that goes on the stage. My grandmother—my mother's mother—was an actress, quite well-known once—Margaret Shirley."

"I remember her," said Cheveril. "She was a good actress, though I think that probably you'll be a better one."

"She came from Australia," Ann continued, pink with pleasure. "And *her* grandfather, who went out to Australia about eighteen-fifty, had worked in the Theatre, though he wasn't famous or anything."

"And what was *his* name?"

"Oh—you wouldn't have ever heard of him. His name was Kettle—Walter Kettle. Why, what's the matter?"

"Nothing. Perhaps I oughtn't to be smoking." He leaned forward, to crush his cigarette into the ashtray, and the hand that held the cigarette was shaking. He felt she was staring at him, and glanced across at her. She was staring at his shaking hand, and when he withdrew it sharply, she raised her eyes to his.

"He never came back," she said slowly. "I believe, in fact, he didn't live very long."

"No, I don't suppose he did."

"But you can't ever have heard of him, Mr. Cheveril. He wasn't a writer or even an actor of any importance."

"Walter Kettle was a stage-manager," Cheveril told her. "He was the stage-manager of this theatre once."

"Are you sure?"

Was he sure? He decided that he was. "Yes, he was here a year or two before he went to Australia. With a manager called Ludlow. There's a little book here that I was looking at," he added hastily, wondering if he was not saying too much, "chiefly about a young actress called Jenny Villiers."

"Why," cried Ann, excited now, "there's a sketch of her. I saw it. Ringlets and things. And it was her glove that was on the floor. A green gauntlet thing, trimmed with red."

He looked at her accusingly. "Now wait a minute. You threw that glove on the floor, didn't you? When I wouldn't talk to you."

She nodded. "Yes, I did. And I remember what I said. I said 'Look—the glove's on the floor again. Even the ghosts are on my side. Be careful.' Yes, that's what I said."

"But why did you say *again?*"

"Because the other time, when I was talking to Miss Fraser, we suddenly saw the glove on the floor. And I said it had jumped out of the case by itself. Miss Fraser pretended it hadn't, but that was because she was frightened. I'd been saying something about that ringlet girl—Jenny Villiers—and then the glove—*her* glove—was there on the floor. Are you all right, Mr. Cheveril?"

"I think so. Why?"

"You're so white."

"I feel a bit white," Cheveril confessed, "but there's really nothing wrong with me. Go on."

"Well, that's all. Except that I understand now why the place seemed so ghosty to me, the moment I really took a look at it. You see, Mr. Cheveril, some of me—the Walter Kettle part—has been here before and knows it quite well. Probably that's why gloves jump out of cases. It was recognising the Walter Kettle bit of me. Oh—I'm so glad you told me about him being here. I'm sure that's why I've been feeling so peculiar. And you have too, haven't you?"

"Yes."

"I knew you had, though of course you aren't well and that may account for it in your case."

"It might," he replied shortly.

She bent towards him, confidentially, and lowered her voice. "You know, we've been giving each other very peculiar looks, haven't we?"

"I didn't know whether mine were, but some of yours were distinctly peculiar." He smiled at her, clearly dismissing the subject. "Now—do you think I could have a look at your Robert?"

"Of course. He'd adore it. His name's Peak—and he's a Wing-Commander."

Cheveril telephoned from the desk to ask that Wing-Commander Peak, now waiting at the stage door, should be sent up to the Green Room. Then he looked at Ann. "Was he an actor?"

She shook her head. "He's never had anything to do with the Theatre. But loves it, of course."

"Are you sure he does?"

"Oh—yes." She was very emphatic. "It would be hopeless if he didn't. By the way, he'll probably be rather shy. He nearly died of shame and misery when I said I wasn't going to be stopped by anybody but meant to see you somehow. They don't do things like that in the Air Force. He saw you as a kind of Air-Marshal sitting here in grandeur."

Cheveril smiled. "Well, I hope you don't."

"Oh no. I didn't like you—and was terribly

174

disappointed—when you turned me away without looking at me. But now of course it's quite different. Because you're quite different too." And she smiled at him confidently.

"Wing-Commander Peak here, Mr. Cheveril," said Otley at the door.

And then Cheveril gasped, and once again felt an icy hand touching his spine. For Julian Napier had entered the room.

20

STILL staring, Cheveril got up and walked across to him. It was no hallucination. When all allowance had been made for the Air Force uniform, the browner face and shorter hair, and the cleaner trimmer look of the young man, this might be Julian Napier over again. The likeness was astonishing. Cheveril looked earnestly from him to Ann, not saying a word.

The young man naturally misinterpreted this behaviour. "I'm sorry," he stammered. "I thought —I mean—they told me to barge in——"

Cheveril came out of his trance. "Yes, yes, of course. That's all right."

Ann came nearer. "This is Robert," she announced proudly, and smiled at her wonderful possession.

"I thought I must be butting in—or something——" Robert muttered, throwing her an agonised glance. His face was now a brick-red and damp with the sweat of embarrassment.

"No, no, my dear chap," cried Cheveril, smiling. "My fault entirely. I'm sorry. I asked them to send you up. Only—you reminded me of somebody, that's all. Er——?" And he hesitated.

"Yes, sir?"

"I was going to ask what other names there are in your family besides Peak——"

"Well, sir——"

"No, it doesn't matter now, thanks. He waited a moment, and took a graver tone. "What does matter though is that this young woman of yours is an actress."

"And wizard, sir, believe me!" cried Robert, six foot of shining enthusiasm.

Cheveril smiled. "Well, if she's not wizard now, perhaps she's going to be. But you realise what that means—that she's not only going to work in the Theatre—but also talk Theatre, eat and drink Theatre, dream Theatre—for years and years?"

Robert grinned. "I've found that out already."

"I warned you right at the very first, darling," said Ann, not without a touch of complacency.

"I'll say you did."

"But you realise too what that means?" Cheveril persisted gently.

"I told her," said Robert, almost on parade, "right at the beginning too, sir, that that was absolutely okay with me—and I meant it too. All I want is for her to do the grand things she can do in the Theatre and I'll just stay in the background and try to look after her."

"Darling!" cried Ann, pink and proud.

"I've no doubt you mean it," said Cheveril, "but it won't be easy—and after you're married——"

But they would not let him continue. "We shall have to tell him," said Ann.

"Go on," Robert said to her.

"You see, we are married. We were married last year."

Cheveril looked at them. "Then it may work out—*this* time." It was out before he could check himself.

They stared at him. "What?"

"I mean," he said, smiling, "I must congratulate you both."

He was shaking hands with them when Pauline entered, hurriedly and in some agitation.

178

"Martin," she began, "I've just heard that you collapsed and had to have the doctor again——"

"All over now, thank you, Pauline. This is Wing-Commander Peak—Miss Pauline Fraser. It seems these two are married. A secret, but I've just prised it out of them."

Pauline shook hands with Robert. "How nice!" And she might have said more but the telephone interrupted her. She looked enquiringly at Cheveril, who nodded and then went to the desk.

It was George Gavin, who began by asking him how he was feeling now and how the ghosts were behaving.

"I think perhaps you owe them something, George," Cheveril told him, and glancing across the room he saw that Pauline, with the two youngsters silent by her side, was looking curiously at him and making no pretence not to be listening with some urgency. "But never mind about that just now. I've changed my mind. I'm going to say *Yes* if your offer's still open."

George sounded delighted. "Of course it is, old man. The one thing I want—and have wanted all through the deal—is for you to come in with me, with as much or as little as you like."

"If you want me to," said Cheveril emphatically, "I'll come in with every penny I possess, George. And give the scheme all the time I have."

179

"That's great news, old man," said George. "Could we get together tomorrow on it?"

"No, I can't," Cheveril told him. "But give me a few days—and you'll have to allow me that, because I'm going to re-write my Third Act and there'll be a hell of a lot to do here—and then I'll have a plan for us, and we can talk the whole thing out."

That would do for George, who set the line crackling with his enthusiastic response.

"All right then, George. No more now. But I'll see you on the First Night here. 'Bye."

Turning to meet the waiting group, he felt rather self-conscious. Pauline, her eyes very bright, came across to meet him.

"Martin, I couldn't help hearing," she said. "Did you mean all that?"

"Yes, and a lot more." He grinned at her, a trifle shyly, feeling oddly young.

"Darling," Ann cried to her Robert, whose embarrassment had started all over again, "we ought to go." She turned expectantly to Cheveril.

"Where did you say this Repertory Company of yours is?" he asked her, smiling.

"Wanley. Not too far from here. Will you come to see me? Will you?" She almost danced.

He nodded. "As soon as I've finished here. And then—well, I might have an idea or two for you."

180

"Gosh!" she cried, so explosively that they all laughed. Then she turned impulsively to Pauline. "He *is* quite different, you know. *Something* happened."

Pauline flashed an enquiring glance at Cheveril, but he was not ready to deal with it yet. Hastily he turned to Robert, and shook his hand. "Good-bye. And you keep on looking after her."

"I promise. Good-bye, sir."

Ann held out her hand to Cheveril. "I'm very, very grateful." She stopped, and looked mischievous. "If I weren't, I think I'd be angry with you." And with an instinctive feeling for a good exit, she moved at once towards the door.

Cheveril was surprised. "Why?"

She swung round at the door, gave him a last look, and then said, in a tone just loud enough to reach him: "Because—and this would make any woman angry—all the time you've kept on looking at me as if you were trying to see somebody else."

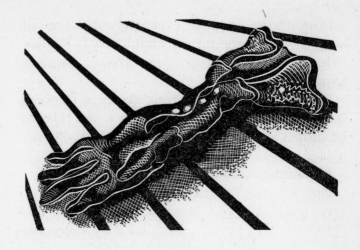

21

P AULINE and he were alone, very much alone,
just as they had been, only an hour or two earlier,
when he had told her he had done with the
Theatre and she had been so angry with him. She
was looking at him now, enquiringly, and he met
the challenge of her fine dark eyes, and then smiled
at her. He was fond of Pauline, devoted to her.
And he suddenly realised that she meant quite as
much to him as he did to her. She had done a lot
for him in the Theatre. They were old troupers
together, with scores of adventures, comic or

desperate, in playhouses in the West End or on the road or in America, piled up behind them, a little stage of their own. But it would be difficult to talk to her again to-night, after what had happened to him. She was too much of his own world and had known him too long, and although nobody would be more enthusiastic than she would be about his change of mind and heart concerning the Theatre, her very presence, the very look of enquiry she was giving him now, made any reasonable explanation of that change impossible. Merely wondering what to say to her made him doubt and shrink and begin pretending even to himself.

"What did the girl mean by that last remark?" she demanded.

"I'm not quite sure," he replied carefully. Then he took a chance, and added: "But I used to know a relative of hers—a chap called Walter Kettle."

To his relief, she accepted this without comment, changing the subject. "And you've accepted George Gavin's offer—and you're staying in the Theatre?"

"Yes. In fact, I'll work harder in it than I've done for a long time. George's hold on those theatres gives us a great chance. We'll try to build up two good permanent companies—find some new talent for 'em—train some promising youngsters, both writers and players. And we'll need your advice and help, Pauline."

She sparkled with pleasure. "Of course, Martin. As soon as this play's on, let's talk about it. You'd rather not start now, I imagine, from what I heard you say to George."

"You're quite right. Cigarette?"

She looked hard at him above the box he held between them. "But why have you changed your mind? What's happened?"

While he put down the box and then gave her a light, he had a moment or two in which to consider his reply. "I've been thinking about the Theatre." He motioned her to the chair near his, and then sat down himself. "I mean, about the Theatre being life in miniature, as the old writers—especially Shakespeare—were always saying."

She gave him an impatient glance. "I know. All the world's a stage—and so on. Everybody acts a part—and so forth. Rather obvious stuff, I've always thought it."

"I wonder," he said slowly, watching the smoke twist and curl, thin out and fade. "I wonder. One man in his time plays many parts. The man is distinct from the parts, and his time is the stage on which he plays them. Is it so obvious, Pauline? If it has been to you, it hasn't to me."

"What isn't obvious about it?" She was no longer impatient, because she saw now that he was

184

serious and was not merely refusing to answer her original question.

"You're wearing your Intelligent Listener face now," he told her, grinning.

"Oh—shut up! No, I mean—go on. And be serious, Martin. It isn't fair if you're not, because I know very well you're not really feeling like clowning. You're dead serious underneath. Aren't you?"

He nodded. "Let's look at it like this. Do you remember how we've often wondered why we take this rum business of make-believe so seriously? We'd work away at it through illness, air-raids, crises in our private lives, not allowing anything to stop us. We've talked about that, and never found any reason—publicity, money, fame, pride— quite good enough. Eh?"

"Yes, I remember, of course. But it could be all of the reasons added together," she said thoughtfully. "I think we decided that, the very last time we talked about it."

"I'd forgotten. But it could, of course. But it might be that there's another reason, quite different—that the whole business is symbolic, and that unconsciously we all recognise that fact."

"I'm not good on the symbolic, Martin. Try something else."

"I believe now," he began earnestly, "that in our

185

life, as in the Theatre, the scenery and costumes and character make-ups and props are only a shadow show, to be packed up and put away when the performance is over. And what is real, indestructible and enduring is all that so many fools imagine to be flimsy and fleeting—the innermost and deepest feelings—the way an honest artist sees his work—the root and heart of a real personal relationship—the flame. Yes, the flame burning clear."

She was startled, and looked at him wide-eyed. "Why did you say it—I mean, about the flame—like that? Martin, what's happened?"

He ignored her question, and continued, with more warmth: "Pauline, for all our vulgar mess of paint and canvas and lights and advertisement, we who work in the Theatre, just because it's a living symbol of the mystery of life, we help to guard and to show the flame." Deliberately he took a lighter tone. "Silly as we look, my dear, we're the servants of the divine secret."

"When I tried to say something like that," she cried, "in my speech to the mayor, you laughed at me."

"I was wrong. And I apologise," he added, as he got up. "And now I must do some work."

She stood up too, and looked delighted. "The Third Act?"

"The Third Act. I've got one or two ideas—and I must make some notes. Mind you, it's not a question of making it softer and easier for the customers. I'm as much against that now as I was before, probably rather more so. But I want to make it truer."

"But what can you do for those people of yours?" she demanded. "You remember what you said? No real understanding. No genuine communication. All mumbling and making frantic gestures behind glass doors."

"I'll fling some of those doors open for them. I'll show at least one or two of them that communication may reach farther and understanding go deeper than—than many of us ever dreamt. I've got to take that risk."

"What risk? What do you mean?"

He smiled, and made a gesture vaguely indicating the desk that waited for him. "No, Pauline."

"All right, I'm going. And I'll tell Bernard not to touch the Third Act to-night and that you might have a new last scene ready for him to-morrow."

"Thank you, Pauline." He saw her move towards the door, and so made at once for the desk. There was some of his scribbling paper there, and he picked it up. He decided then that he would work in the armchair. Somehow he did not want to sit at the desk, with a businesslike back turned to the room. He must look at the room and not turn his back on it. But Pauline had not gone. She was standing just inside the door.

"Martin, *what happened?*"

He shook his head at her. "I took four tablets instead of two."

"That's not all. Something happened."

"No, my dear, don't press me," he said, sitting down. "I doubt if I can take it."

"Will you tell me sometime?"

"I'll try. But it'll be difficult. What I felt was intensely real—and that's why I'm ready to take the risk of opening those doors—but the rest of it—well, it might have been a dream—or delirium—or——"

"Or what? That's not all."

"Probably it is. Enough now, Pauline."

"That's cowardly of you," she said with some warmth. She had left the door and had come several paces nearer him. "You felt it—and it's changed you. Or what—then?"

"Oh—well," he replied very slowly, not looking at her, "communication and understanding outside our time, somewhere on the other side of things, where people aren't so separate as they think—no, I can't say any more, my dear."

"All right," she said softly, "I won't ask now."

And in her quick graceful way, she came across, put a hand on his shoulder lightly, and kissed him. Then she looked rather stern. "But don't go back on whatever it was."

"I don't want to. You pop off and do some work."

"I'm going to. You half look to me," she continued eyeing him speculatively, "as if you've suddenly discovered you're in love with somebody. And I think that's what the Seward girl meant by her parting remark."

"Then you're both wrong. It's much more complicated than that. Or even simpler," he added. "In love with life perhaps. Having come out of the dry wilderness. I promise to try and tell you sometime, Pauline. If I can sort it out, and don't feel that I've been fooling myself."

"Why should you have been?"

"I can't help remembering the sceptical grin on that doctor's face. He's seen people like me before."

"Doctors don't know everything." Which was a fine sturdy declaration from Pauline, who had a habit of flying from one end of Harley Street to the other if she felt a mere tickling in the throat.

"No, but they get about a bit." Then he continued in a lower voice: "And I've no proof. There can't be any proof now."

"You're the proof," she said softly. "What more do you want?"

"I don't know. I don't know anything just now. That's why I don't want to talk."

"Well, don't let go, Martin—and be unhappy again."

When she had gone he was far from feeling unhappy again, but he did find himself lost in a mood of sombre bewilderment. He set the pad of scribbling paper on his knee but found it impossible to concentrate on his notes for the revision of the Third Act. Delighted to welcome any excuse, he decided that there was too much light in the room. It was like trying to work in some glaring third-rate museum. He marched across to the door near Otley's office, and switched off most of the lights, just leaving his own corner fully illuminated. And now once again this was the Green Room where it had happened. But where *what* had happened? And why feel an idiotic sense of loss when he had not a shadow of proof that anything had ever really happened? Oh—either accept the whole daft business—or reject and have done with it! But he found he could do neither, and sat lumped in his chair, unable to work, at once indecisive, bewildered, and angry with himself. And then a flash of scarlet, with some olive green near it, caught his eye, and brought him up out of his chair, all bewilderment, doubt, self-contempt burned away.

The glove was on the floor again.

THE END